GHOST TOWN MYSTERY

Frank Austin

WESTBOW
PRESS®
A DIVISION OF THOMAS NELSON
& ZONDERVAN

WestBow Press books may be ordered through booksellers or by contacting:

WestBow Press
A Division of Thomas Nelson & Zondervan
1663 Liberty Drive
Bloomington, IN 47403
www.westbowpress.com
1 (866) 928-1240

Interior Image Credit: Frank Austin

Scripture taken from the King James Version of the Bible.

ISBN: 978-1-9736-9260-7 (sc)
ISBN: 978-1-9736-9259-1 (e)

Print information available on the last page.

WestBow Press rev. date: 6/15/2020

Books that build
Christian character

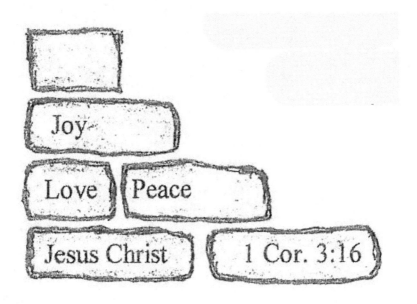

Joy

Love Peace

Jesus Christ 1 Cor. 3:16

Dedicated to my wife, my children, and my grandchildren, and friends who encouraged me to complete this book.

CONTENTS

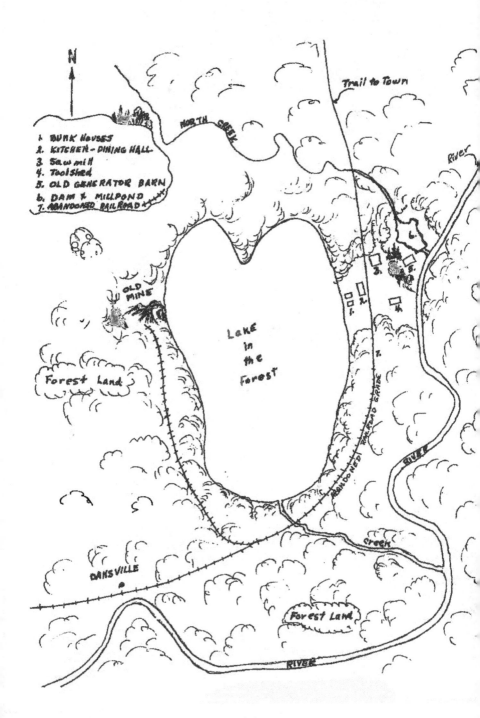

CHAPTER I
STRANGE SOUNDS

The underbrush was thick, but Gil forced his body through it. *Like trying to push a lineman aside at football practice*, he thought. Good thing they didn't have far to go.

Just behind him, his friend Jug complained, "Hey, Gil don't go so fast, I can't keep up." Jug who was short and heavy set, was no match for Gil when it came to walking in heavy brush.

"We do have to hurry," Lori called from behind.

"Won't be long before the sun goes down and we don't want to get caught out here after sundown, do we, Ann?"

Gil looked back at the girls. Lori was tall and blond. His cousin Ann, was dark haired and smaller. While neither one was timid, they had spoken the truth. They were surrounded by thousands of acres of wilderness and none of them wanted to be caught out in the woods overnight.

Gil turned and pushed into the brush. Just ahead, almost completely hidden by the forest was an ancient building. It was part of an abandoned logging camp that was being converted into a camp for troubled inner-city kids. It had remained undisturbed in a remote area of Michigan's Upper Peninsula for many years. But now, after discovering it earlier that afternoon, Gil was anxious to do some exploring.

His thoughts flashed back over the past couple of weeks. He had wanted to work at home this summer to earn some money for college. But then his plans had changed when Jim West had asked him to come help at the old lumber camp. Jim was his favorite uncle and he hated to turn him down. Then there was Lori. *I don't want to be away from her all summer,* Gil thought. *She's very special.*

Yes, it had been a hard decision to make. But a week earlier when the canoes headed down the river toward the secluded camp, the excitement had pushed his doubts far back into his mind and now he was enjoying the adventure to the fullest.

"Hey, there it is," Gil pointed toward a dark shadow in the trees, then turned and called back, "I hope this place isn't haunted. I hear those loggers were pretty tough guys!" He quickly turned his head to hide the smile that betrayed the concern in his voice.

"You guys are just trying to scare us," Lori laughed. "Besides, a ghost wouldn't keep you long when he saw how much YOU guys eat."

Gil moved on to the brush-covered building where tall maple and birch trees shut out much of the late afternoon sun. "Let's start at this corner and see if we can find a door before it gets too dark," he suggested, motioning for the others to spread out along the building.

"Hey, I found it," Jug called moments later. He pulled a hatchet from his belt and began to chop away at the brush. Soon a weathered door secured by a rusty padlock appeared in the opening.

Gill grabbed an armload of discarded branches and tossing

them away he said, "We're going to need that wrecking bar that you have, Lori."

Taking the bar, he hooked it behind the lock and pulled. His arm muscles bulged as he strained against the lock, but it didn't move.

"Give me a hand, Jug," he grunted.

Jug's hands reached out and together they pulled against the stubborn lock, but nothing moved. Jug eased off the bar slightly and then jerked with all his might. A split second later wood began to splinter and the lock popped off the door and fell at their feet.

Gil handed the bar back to Lori and reached for the doorknob. Suddenly, an eerie screeching sound came from overhead, and he froze in his tracks.

"What was that?" Jug cried and backed away from the door.

The girls paused, motionless, listening intently for the sound, but only the noise of the forest creatures greeted their ears. Then the spine chilling screee-cchh came again from high in the trees.

Ann grabbed her cousin's arm and whispered, "Do you think someone is in there?"

"Don't know what it is," Gil whispered. "Never heard anything like that before." Just then, the sound of brush cracking came from the trees behind them. "Something's coming," he spoke softly, just as another screee---cchh sounded overhead.

Gil's heart pounded so hard he was sure the others could hear it.

Then another branch crackled and a familiar voice called, "Where are you guys?"

"Oh, it's just Uncle Jim coming to help us," Gil heaved a sigh of relief

"We've been hearing strange sounds up there," Ann pointed as her father stepped up beside them.

Gil took a couple of steps back and studied the side of the building. Screee---cchh, the sound came again. His eyes moved higher and he felt a slight breeze on his face. Screee---cchh. "Oh I see what's making the noise," he motioned. "See that branch up there? It's rubbing on the side of the building and it screeches every time the wind moves the top of the tree."

"Oh, that's a relief," Lori sighed. "I was almost beginning to believe in ghosts."

"OK, now that we've got that settled, let's see what's inside," Uncle Jim suggested.

Gil reached for the knob. It turned, but the door didn't move. He raised his other hand and pushed but it still wouldn't give.

"Hold the knob and let me at it," Jug commanded and stepped back several steps. He lowered his shoulder like he was going for a football player twice his size, and lunged at the door. Ker-thud! Squeek---crash! Jug went sprawling inside. Clouds of dust came billowing out the door.

"You all right?" Ann cried out, concern showing in her voice.

"I guess so," Jug moaned and slowly stood to his feet. Gil smiled at the sight. Jug was covered with dust from head to toe, but seemed to be alright otherwise.

"We'll take you down to the lake when we get done here and scrub you down."

"I'll do my own scrubbing, if you don't mind," Jug told them.

Gil turned and stepped inside the building. Boards had been nailed over the windows years earlier, and with the great trees arching over the building, very little light penetrated the inner darkness. "We're going to need a lantern," he called out the door.

"We'll get one," the girls responded and took off on a run toward the dining hall.

"While we're waiting, we may as well get some of these windows uncovered," Uncle Jim suggested. "Maybe we can figure out what this building was used for when the girls get back."

It didn't take long to uncover a couple of windows and by the time they were finished the girls had returned with the gas lanterns. Gil took one and quickly pumped air into the tank, then turned on the gas and lit the mantel. It sputtered and glowed dimly for a moment, then came up to full brightness. Electric power lines were a long ways from the camp, so gas lanterns were very important here in the wilderness.

Gil held the light high and stepped inside. "That's much better," he called back as the light drove the darkness into the far comers. Surveying the room, he saw several piles of lumber that stood near a large door on the right. To his left, a long workbench covered with various tools sat against the wall. Nearby, tall shelves held boxes of nails, bolts, and a variety of hardware. Farther back, a stairway led to a second story. Near the stairway, he noticed what looked like a large electric motor with wires running to a fuse box. A wide belt connected it to a ball bat sized shaft that ran through the back wall.

Gil paused, a frown coming to his brow. "Why is this electric motor here when they didn't have electric power?"

Uncle Jim stepped closer and inspected the motor. Glancing around the room, he told them, "Look there." He pointed toward several light fixtures hanging around the room and said, "I think this must be a generator!"

"You think so?" Jug asked. "Boy, wouldn't it be great if we could make it work!"

"Sure would be," Uncle Jim agreed, "it'd save us a lot of money."

"Hey, let's go see where that shaft goes," Gil motioned to Jug.

Outside, the ground dropped off quickly as they approached the back of the building. "Look, there's a creek down there in the trees," Gil pointed. Moving farther around the backside, he discovered an eight foot high stone wall and a brush covered ridge of dirt running farther back into the trees. "This doesn't look quite natural," he observed.

"I'm going to see where this ridge goes," he reached out and pulled the brush back so he could squeeze through. Suddenly he caught his toe on something and went sprawling on the ground. "Ooh," he moaned and looked back to see what had tripped him.

"Hey," he called. "That shaft we saw in the building comes through here. I just tripped over it."

Getting to his feet, he followed the shaft away from the building. He had only gone a few feet when the embankment stopped with a stone wall and an eight foot drop to the creek below. Pulling a branch out of the way, he discovered a wheel-shaped rusty steel framework fastened to the shaft. Glancing to the other side, he saw another stone wall with the end of the shaft resting on the top of it.

"Where are you, Jug?" he called.

"Right here," Jug answered from below and to the left. "What's up?"

"Looks like the remains of a water wheel," Gil explained.

"The creek's here," Jug noted. "Do you think this was a dam to power the generator?"

Jug was not as athletic as Gil, but he knew Jug had a good natural understanding of mechanical things. At a time like this, he was a good friend to have around.

Gil studied the framework of the wheel. "I think you're right, Jug. It does appear to be the remains of a dam."

Jug squeezed through the brush and appeared in an open spot just below Gil. He paused to look at the wheel and then spoke, "Looks like wooden boxes were fastened here to catch water and turn the wheel," he pointed. "Then the wheel turns the shaft and the shaft turns the generator. Simple, huh. Do you think we could make it work?"

"Well, we've got lots of boards and bolts inside this building," Gil replied. "The waterway seems to be made of concrete, and look, there's the steel framework for the gate to close off the water. We'll have to put some boards on it, but that shouldn't be any big problem for us."

"I think you're right," Jug agreed. "If we get this brush cleared out of here, we could fix it in no time."

"Let's go tell the others," Gil nodded and began to make his way back through the brush.

Later, Gil turned and took one last look at the lake. He drank in the beauty of the forest reflected on the glassy surface of the water as the sun slipped behind the great maples on the opposite shore. The water was cool and refreshing, but it was getting late. Just time to get changed and grab a snack.

Gil settled down next to Uncle Jim as he picked up his Bible and began to read; "Consider the lilies of the field, how they grow; they toil not, neither do they spin: and yet I say unto you, That even Solomon in all his glory was not arrayed like one of these."

Gil's mind flashed back to the lilies growing in his yard back home. He loved the beauty of the flowers. He marveled at the flaming sunsets and roaring waterfalls.

"---For all these things do the nations of the world seek after." Jim continued reading. "And your Father knows that you have need of all these things."

Gil's thoughts turned to his needs. Money had been scarce. The decision to come north for the summer had been difficult. It had been a great opportunity, but it wouldn't provide anything for his college fund.

"For where your treasure is, there will your heart be also," Jim finished reading.

What does that mean? Gil thought as he and Jug headed for the bunk house. *I really don't have any treasure. If I had a lot of money and kept it all for myself, I could understand. But can God really provide for me when I don't have a job?*

Gil stretched and settled down in his bunk. His thoughts turned to the people who had lived and worked at this camp

Frank Austin

in years gone by. Drifting off into sleep, he dreamed that the camp was alive with people. He wanted to ask them some questions, but when he approached someone, they seemed to always disappear just before he could speak. He was feeling very frustrated. Then suddenly, he awoke.

CHAPTER II
THE MYSTERIOUS JAR

ew dripped from the trees and the early morning sun bad turned the sky to glowing gold. Songbirds of the forest were singing their wakeup calls while inside the boy's bunkhouse, a strange noise roused Gil. Still half asleep, he couldn't imagine what it might be until his hand found a flashlight and turned it in the direction of the noise. "Oh, that's it," he muttered. ''Should have recognized Jug's snore."

He checked his watch. *Five o'clock, soon be time to get up.*

Forty five minutes later, Gil could see smoke rising from the chimney as he and Jug headed for the dining hall. Inside, Aunt Mary was stirring pancake batter, and the aroma of bacon frying on the cook stove awoke his appetite. "Good morning," he greeted the girls as they all met at the kitchen door.

Stepping inside, Gil called, "Aunt Mary, would you like me to fry the pancakes?''

"If you'd like to," she answered.

"I'll go to the spring to get the milk," Jug volunteered. In this remote area, the ice cold spring water kept their food cool much like a refrigerator.

It wasn't long before Aunt Mary called, "It's ready. Gather around the table and Jim will give thanks for the food."

A couple of minutes later Ann's voice broke the silence, "Did you see that?"

"See what?" Lori asked.

"Jug ate a whole pancake in one bite! I didn't think anyone, not even Jug, could get a whole pancake in his mouth at once, let alone chew it up and swallow it."

Jug swallowed quickly and took a big drink of milk. "It was just a little one, and I was starving!" he protested, then rolled up another pancake and stuffed it into his mouth.

It was just past 7 o'clock when breakfast was done and Uncle Jim finished with devotions. He stood up and said, "It's a good thing we got the trail opened up out to the road last week. We're going to need some power tools and a generator to repair the dam and Mary and the girls need some groceries from town. While we're gone to get the things, you fellows can start cutting some of the brush back there around the dam, if you'd like to."

An hour later Gil paused to look around. It was much easier to see, now that most of the brush was cleared away from the dam. Rusty chains held the steel framework of the old gate suspended over the creek. He reached out and grabbed a spoke of the water wheel and gave a tug, but it didn't move. "Would you give me a hand?" he called to Jug.

"Sure," Jug replied. "Let me at it." The two boys pushed against the spokes with all their might, but it only moved a few inches. "I think we'd better get some oil in the bearings and try it later," he suggested.

"Good idea," Gil responded. While you do that, I'm going to

find some boards to fix the gate. We need to get that repaired first so the water can be building up in the dam."

Gil took a tape measure from his belt and checked the gate for size, then headed around to the front of the building. The lumber piles they had found inside were going to come in handy. The former owners of the sawmill bad left behind some very nice boards, he discovered as he sorted through the pile. Sliding one last board out the doorway, Gil spoke to himself, "There, I think that ought to do it. Now to get them around in back."

He picked up a stack of boards and headed outside. As he rounded the comer of the building he met Jug coming toward him.

"I got the bearings oiled," Jug told him. "Let's let the oil work down into the bearings and we'll try it again in a few minutes."

"Sounds good," Gil answered back. "If you want to grab the chainsaw, I'll get these boards marked for length." He began stacking the boards evenly on two blocks of wood, then returned to get the rest of them.

Gil was almost done when Jug returned with the saw. "We'll have to cut the rough ends off so they'll be square," he told him Placing the last board in place, He took a square and put a mark across the top near the end, then put another mark down the side of the pile.

"All set," he said softly and reached for the saw.

With a couple of sharp pulls on the starting rope, the saw roared to life. While Jug steadied the pile, Gil carefully touched the chain to the boards and a shower of chips flew to the ground as the saw cut through the boards. Only a few seconds later, the rough ends fell away from the pile and Gil moved to the other end to make the final cut.

Just as the saw grew silent, Gil heard Uncle Jim's voice call from the corner of the building, "How are you coming?"

"We got the brush out of the way and the boards cut to repair the gate," Jug responded.

"Now we're ready for the generator and a drill," Gil added. "We'll give you a hand getting the generator around here."

Uncle Jim spoke as they headed to get the tools, "While you guys work on the gate, I'm going to do some cleaning and service work on the old generator inside. After all these years, it probably needs some checking out before we try to run it."

Returning to the dam, they set the tools down, and Jim inspected the waterway for a moment. "If you put a couple of boards across those rocks, you can walk on them without getting your feet wet."

"Good idea," Gil replied as Lori and Ann came around the corner of the building.

"Is there something we can do?" Lori called.

"Sure," Gill replied. "We'll get the generator started and put some boards on the gate."

"I'll hold a board in place, and Jug, you drill the holes for the bolts. You girls can put the bolts in the holes and screw the nuts on them."

"Let us at it,' Jug commanded and touched the drill to the wood. Shavings flew and fell to the creek below, and a second later the drill bit popped through the other side. "This one is done," he announced and moved to the other end.

Picking a bolt from a wooden box, Lori pushed it through the hole, while on the other side, Ann spun a nut on the end of it. Meanwhile, Jug completed the second hole and the girls repeated the process.

Twenty minutes later, Gil lifted a board up to the top of the gate. "This is the last one we'll have to bolt on the gate. After this, we need to nail another layer of boards on so the joints are mismatched with the first layer. That way, the joints won't be so apt to leak water.

Finally, the last board was nailed in place and Jug called, "Are we ready to let it down?"

"I think so," Gil replied. "I'll see if I can get the gate to move." He scrambled up the bank and grabbed a plastic bottle of oil. "I'm going to oil all the joints on this thing," he told them. "Looks like it needs all the help we can give it."

He set the bottle of oil down when he was finished and grabbed the big crank giving it a pull. "Ahh, it won't move," he groaned.

Jug pointed to the gear. "There's a catch there to hold it up." He picked up a hammer and carefully tapped the catch until he dislodged it from the gear. "There, now if we can just get this shaft to turn, we'll be all set." Gil gave the crank another pull and Jug gave it two sharp blows with the hammer. "Hey, it moved!" Gil cried out.

"I'll get down below and keep watch," Jug told him as the gate began to inch downward.

"I'm going to put a little more oil on the gears," Gil suggested.

Jug scrambled down the bank and Gil began to lower the gate once more. With each tum, the crank moved more freely and the gate dropped lower until it was about a foot above the creek.

"Wait a minute," Jug bent down to pull the boards that spanned the creek out of the way, then called, "Let her down a little more."

"I need a shovel," Jug called. "Hold it up a minute until I get these sticks and stones on the creek bottom out of the way." Taking the shovel, he quickly scraped the rubble downstream from the gate and ordered, "Let her down."

Gil slowly lowered the gate until it settled firmly on the concrete strip in the bottom of the stream.

"Look," Ann pointed. "There's hardly any water coming through now."

"And it's beginning to back the water up behind it already," Lori commented.

Just then, Gil heard the ding dong of the big dinner bell ringing through the trees. "We got done just in time! Let's go eat."

"We've been so busy, I didn't even notice that I was hungry," Jug spoke up. " But now that I think about it, I am really hungry."

Jug's eyes swept over the table. "Potatoes and gravy, baked beans, and hot apple pie. Not bad for a first course. Gil, hurry up and ask the blessing before I starve to death."

Gil smiled. Jug sure did like to eat. *Guess we'd better get started with dinner, cause we 've got a water wheel to repair this afternoon,* he thought as he bowed his head to ask the blessing.

Later, Jug stuffed a big bite of apple pie in his mouth and called, "Aunt Mary, I'm getting too full for the second course now, could you bring it out to us in a couple of hours?"

"Sorry," Aunt Mary replied, "But this restaurant doesn't deliver. You'll have to come and get it. However, I will do the dishes for all of you since you're trying to get electricity for my kitchen."

"Ok. If that's the way you feel about it," Jug smiled. "Well, if you two are done negotiating, we'd better get back at our work," Uncle Jim suggested sliding back from the table. "Let's get the table cleared and then head for the woods."

Back at the dam, Lori stepped up beside Gil and pointed, "Look, the water is half way up on the gate already."

"Yes it is," Gil agreed. "The first part will fill quickly, but the last few feet will take a lot longer because it spreads out over a lot bigger area."

Just then Uncle Jim came around the comer of the building and called, "I made a pattern this morning for the boxes to go on the water wheel." he held up a wooden box and placed it on the frame of the wheel.

"Yes, that should fit like it's supposed to," he nodded and said, "We'll need to make enough of these to go all the way around the water wheel."

"There's a couple of saw horses in the building," Gil told the others. "If we put some boards across them, we can make a table to work on." He was proud of his friends. They made a good team and an hour later, a stack of boxes were all ready to bolt on to the water wheel.

"Boy, Jug, you must have done a good job of oiling this wheel." Gil spoke as he gave the wheel a pull. "It turns quite easily now." The four teens went to work bolting the boxes in place and by mid afternoon the job was finished.

"What now Uncle Jim?" Gil questioned.

Jim came over to inspect the repairs they had made, then replied, "It went much faster than I though it would. It'll save a lot of time and money if this generator will work. I have to go make a couple of phone calls in town, so I can take back the tools we rented when I go. I'd like to see if the generator is going to work before we make too many more plans. If you take care of the tools you guys can have the rest of the afternoon off."

"Hey, that sounds like a great idea," Gil wiped the sweat from his forehead. "I'm ready for a swim! How about you guys?"

"What are we waiting for?" Jug cried. "Let's take care of these tools and go get changed."

Gil paused in the shade to wait for the others. His eyes swept over the lake sparkling in the afternoon sun. Their homemade raft, an old barn door tied across two canoes, rocked gently in the glistening water. It looked so inviting. Hearing the girl's voices, he turned to see Jug shuffling behind them, his face mask dangling from his hand.

Suddenly, he darted around the girls and called, "Last one in is a rotten egg!"

"Watch out for a tidal wave," Gil warned the girls as Jug hit the water. Gil leaped into the lake and swam toward the canoes. "That sure cools you off in a hurry,' he called to Jug as he pulled himself up on the raft. He hesitated only long enough to pull Lori up and then dove in again. The water felt a little warmer, now that he was beginning to get used to it.

As he swam deeper into the crystal clear water, he could see water logged pieces of wood laying here and there on the sandy bottom. Something caught his eye off to the left. Swimming closer, he picked up a blood red stone the size of a golf ball. *Pretty*, he thought. *I'll take it up with me.* He raised his hands and pushed toward the surface, then swam to the raft. Pulling himself up beside Lori who sat on the edge of the raft, he examined the stone. "I guess it's nothing special," he observed turning the stone in his fingers. "Just a pretty stone."

Looking over Gil's shoulder, Jug called, "Toss it back in the water and let's see who can find it first."

"Good idea," Ann agreed.

The water boiled as the four teens dove in. Ann was the first to spot it and quickly grabbing it, she headed for the surface.

After the stone had been tossed out and retrieved many times, Lori challenged them, "You guys make it too easy," then gave the stone a toss into deeper water.

Gil dove in toward the ripples. Here, the bottom dropped off quickly. His eyes searched the sand. *Where is that stone?* Off to his left he saw Jug reach out and pick something off the bottom, then head for the surface. He was about to head up too, when he noticed something that didn't look natural. The object was round and long like a block of firewood.

I'm getting low on air, he thought. *But maybe I can get it closer to the raft.* He reached out for the object but it was slippery and heavy, hard to hang on to. Grabbing it with both hands, he clutched it to his side like a large football and headed for the surface. Suddenly, he felt breathless, overwhelmed. *I'm not going to make it in time. Got to have air!* He dropped the object and kicked with all his might, then just as his lungs were about to burst, his head cleared the surface and gasped in several deep breaths of air.

I'd better not cut it so close next time, he thought.

He took one more deep breath and headed for the bottom again. Reaching it, he scooped up the object, then with a great leap he headed up toward the surface. He could only swim with one arm now, and the extra weight kept trying to pull him back under. *Man, this thing is heavy, but I don't want to drop it again.* Then, just as his lungs were screaming for another breath of air, his head cleared the surface and someone dove in beside him. It was Jug.

"Give me a hand," he begged.

Moving close, Gil felt Jug's hand grab the back of his swimming trunks and pull him toward the raft. One thing about Jug, he had a lot of natural buoyancy. A couple of seconds later they reached the raft.

"Can I help," Lori called reaching down from the raft.

Gil grabbed a canoe with his free hand, and with a boost from Jug they raised the object up to the girls.

"What is this thing?" Lori questioned. "It's cold and slimy."

"I'm not sure. Probably nothing," Gil answered. "It feels like it might be made of glass," he noted rubbing some of the slime away.

Spotting a tin can in the bottom of one of the canoes, Jug called, "Maybe this will help." He grabbed the can, dipped it in the lake, and began to rinse away some of the dirt.

Suddenly a look of recognition came over Ann's face as she watched. "That's an antique fruit jar like my grandma has in her basement," she told them

The glass cover of the old blue-green jar was secured in place with a wire bail. Gil picked up the jar and held it up toward the sun.

"Hey, you can see outlines through the glass!" Lori pointed.

"Yes, it looks like there might be some coins in it," Gil agreed, excitement showing in his voice. "Let's get this back to the dining hall and see if we can get it open!"

"I'll get a canoe," Lori told them and dove in and swam toward a canoe tied to a tree on the shore.

Gil watched her graceful movements as she untied the canoe, pulled it into the water and headed back to the raft. Moments later she eased the canoe up to the raft.

"Hold it steady," Gil told Jug and Ann as he handed the jar to Lori, then stepped carefully into the canoe.

"We'll swim to shore," Jug spoke up as he pushed the canoe away from the raft. He and Ann then dove in the water and headed for shore.

They all reached land about the same time. Gil stepped out into the shallow water and with Jug's help they pulled the canoe up on the beach and tied it to the tree once more.

"It won't be long before it's time to eat," Gil noted picking the jar from the bottom of the canoe. "Let's get changed and we'll meet in the dining hall. After we eat, we'll see if we can get this thing open."

"What have you got," Aunt Mary inquired as they entered the dining hall.

"We found it in the lake, Gil replied, setting the jar on the table. "We think it might have some coins in it."

"You think so? That sure would be a surprise," she responded. "I expect Uncle Jim to be back anytime. If you guys want to help set the table, we can eat just as soon as he gets here.

Placing the last fork on the table, Jug called, "Uncle Jim just pulled in. Let's get the food on the table!" "What's the big hurry?" Ann spoke up with a big smile on her face.

"I'm about to perish from hunger," he said in a little boy voice.

"You poor thing," Ann said in pretended sympathy. "Here, have a piece of celery."

"I need real food, not that rabbit food," he shot back from the kitchen. "You just can't get any good kitchen help anymore," he sputtered. "A guy could starve to death right in this dining room."

Uncle Jim entered the room and Ann called to him, "We've got to get some food down Jug quick. He's on the verge of starvation."

Jim stopped and eyed the heavy set young man from head to toe. "Well. I guess he *has* just wasted away to skin and bones." He gave Jug a big smile and grabbed him by the arm. "Young man, let's just sit you down here and see if we can nourish you back to life."

After Jim asked the blessing, Jug spoke up, "Aunt Mary, you're sure a good cook. You fix my favorite food every time."

"That's because *any* food is your favorite food," Ann laughed. "You'll eat anything."

"Just don't worry about me," Jug came back pretending his feelings were hurt. "You're just jealous of my taste for fine food."

"Or any other kind of food," Gil countered. Jug had a great sense of humor and the only thing he loved more than food was getting his friends going in one of his unique discussions.

Later, when the tables were cleared, Uncle Jim announced, "I'm going to go check the dam. Maybe we can tell about how long it's going to take before we can try to start the generator."

Gil looked toward Jug. "We'll go too."

The outside air was still warm, but it was much cooler as they moved into the trees. Rounding the comer of the old building Jim called, "Looks like the water is about half way up to where it needs to be." His eyes swept over the pond that was building up behind the dam. Pointing to several large trees he said, "Looks like we need to cut those trees first thing in the morning. The water will come up on them and kill them if we wait until later, and we don't want to have to drain the dam again just to get to the trees."

"Do you think the dam will be full by tomorrow night?" Gil questioned.

"Yes, I think so," Jim replied. "By this time tomorrow, we could have power if that old generator works.„ He took one last look around the then turned, "Let's go see what you guys dragged out of the lake."

Back in the dining hall, the girls had just finished with the dishes and they all gathered at the table where the old jar had been placed earlier.

"Why don't you get a pan of water and a scrub brush," Aunt Mary suggested. "Take it out on the back steps and scrub it down?"

"That's a good idea. I'll get the pan and brush," Jug volunteered and headed for the kitchen.

Gil picked up the jar, then headed outside and set it down on the step. Pulling a jackknife from his pocket and began to scrape away at the dirt.

"Got some warm soapy water," Jug said setting the pan on the step. "Put it in there and I'll wash it."

Gil laid the jar in the pan. "I'll hang on to it while you scrub it," he offered holding the jar firmly with both hands. Moments later, when most of the dirt had been removed, he stood the jar upright and said, "Let's see if we can get some of the rust and dirt off this cover."

Jug scrubbed on it for a couple of minutes then commented, "That's about all I can get. Let's rinse it off and take it inside."

After rinsing the jar, Gil carried it inside and put it on one of the tables. Taking his knife once more, he began scraping away at the wire bail that locked the cover in place. "I don't want to break the bail if I can help it. If we can just get this wire to move, maybe we can get the cover off without breaking anything."

Gil scraped and poked at the wires for several minutes, then laid the knife down. "The bail is pretty thin after the rust is gone, but I guess if it won't give now, we'll just have to break the wires."

Uncle Jim moved close and suggested, "I think if you lift this wire here on the side, it should loosen the one that goes over the top."

Gil picked up a small screwdriver and pried lightly against the wire. At first there was no movement, then he pushed again and called softly, "Hey, this side broke loose." A couple more pries and the bail slipped up loosening the wire that went over the top of the cover.

Gil reached out and slipped the top wire from the cover. "Ok, now we're finally making progress," he commented. Let's see what's inside."

Grasping the cap in his hand, he twisted and wiggled the cover but it didn't move. "Got any ideas, Uncle Jim?"

"It looks like there may be a rubber ring between the cover and the jar," Jim replied. "You'll probably have to force a thin knife blade between the gasket and the top to break the seal. Those old rubber rings could stick pretty tight sometimes."

"Let me try my jackknife," Jug suggested. Opening the smallest blade, he began to poke it in between the cap and the gasket moving it back and forth to make a wider cut. Then pulling it out, he moved it over a quarter inch and repeated the process until he had gone three quarters of the way around the jar.

"Hey, I think it's working," he squealed. "I can feel the cap move a little when I stick the blade in." He poked the blade in several more times and then said, "I think I've about got it." Grabbing the top he twisted and suddenly the cap carne off in his hand.

They gathered around as Gil peered inside. "It looks like

something wrapped in a piece of cloth." He reached out and tried to slip his hand inside, but the neck of the jar was too small.

"Let me try," Lori offered. Reaching out, she slipped her small hand into the jar and pulled out the cloth wrapped object. Laying it on the table, she pulled the cloth from it, and cried out, "Wow, look at this!"

Gil's eyes widened. "A fancy gold watch. It looks just like new." Picking it up, he pushed a button on the winding stem and the engraved face popped open with ease.

"Look, there's something written on the inside of the cover," Lori spoke as she leaned closer.

Gil turned the watch to catch the light, and read, "To Joe Green, for outstanding service to Superior Logging Company. All at once thoughts raced his mind, *Who's Joe Green? What is Superior Logging Company, and why is this jar in the lake?*

"Hey, quit dreaming, and let's see what else is in there," Jug pleaded.

Gil shoved the jar closer to the girls and one by one they began to remove the things. He was amazed as coin after coin was spread before them. Picking up several of them, he checked the dates. "They're old," he suggested, placing them back on the table.

Once again, his mind was racing. As a boy he had collected coins and knew that some of these would be valuable. Silver coins, gold coins, the watch, and the jar wasn't empty yet. *There's enough value to make a big dent in my college expenses for the first year. Maybe Dad was right*, he thought. *But are they mine? Is it really, "Finders keepers?"*

Suddenly, his attention was turned back to the jar just as Lori pulled another cloth wrapped object from it's resting place and unwrapped it. "Oh, look at this, Gil. It's a gold locket!"

With her fingernail, she popped open the cover and Gil leaned close. Inside was the picture of a young woman. "June 10, 1899," she read the date engraved on the cover.

"Wow, that's old," Ann spoke up. "How do you suppose that got in this lake way up in this wilderness area?"

"That's a good question," Gil answered.

Uncle Jim spoke up, "Remember, there was an old copper mine on the other side of the lake, and this old sawmill dates back at least a hundred years. Just because this place has been deserted now for a half century, doesn't mean it has always been that way. Down through the years, a lot of people have used this lake"

"Yes, I guess you're right," Gil replied, trying to imagine the area around them bustling with activity.

Just then Ann announced, "This is the last one," and laid another $20 dollar gold piece on the table.

The room grew silent as the things passed back and forth to be examined. Gil's mind was racing again. *This jar must have been valuable to someone. But who did it belong to, and why was it in the lake?*

"Hey, it's getting dark. Jug broke the silence. "It's nine o'clock already and I haven't had my bedtime snack yet."

"Let's gather these things up and we'll find a safe place to hide them for tonight," Uncle Jim suggested. "We've got a busy morning tomorrow, so we'd better grab a snack and get ready for bed."

"There's a big plastic dish and cover in the kitchen that you can use," Aunt Mary offered. "Just put it behind some of the boxes of food. It should be safe there."

"Thanks, Aunt Mary," Gil picked up the jar and headed for the kitchen.

Six cookies and a glass of milk later, Gil called, "We're heading for bed now. See you all in the morning." He picked up the lantern and headed out the door.

The night air was cool as they walked past the first bunkhouse. That building was separated into two sections. The smaller part that had once been the mill foreman's quarters, was now occupied by Uncle Jim and Aunt Mary. The larger section, which used to be sleeping quarters for sawmill workers, had been taken over by Lori and Ann.

Nearby stood the boys bunkhouse. Just before stepping inside, Gil paused to look at the lake. It mirrored the fading light of the sky, and across the lake trees cast dark shadows on it's glassy surface. *There's nothing that can compare to the beauty of God's creation*, Gil mused.

Stepping up beside his friend, Jug spoke softly, "How could anyone think that this was all just an accident of nature? God's handiwork sure is plain to see here in this forest setting."

"I know what you mean," Gil answered as they turned to go inside.

Gil set the light on a small table as they entered a long room lined with bunks on each side, then quickly prepared for bed. Before turning in, he picked up his Bible and turned to Luke 15, "---what woman having ten pieces of silver, if she lose one piece, does not light a candle, and sweep the house, and seek diligently until she find it?" he read.

As Gil lay in his bunk his thoughts turned to the contents of the jar. *I wonder how that jar got into the lake? Who was the pretty lady in the locket? And who was Joe Green? The newest coins in the jar are over sixty years old. Could their owner still be alive? Not very likely. But still, remotely possible?*

CHAPTER III

SEARCHING FOR CLUES

ood morning!" Gil greeted Lori and joined her as she walked toward the dining hall. "Looks like it's going to be another beautiful day."

"Yes, it does," she gave him a big smile.

Once again the camp was waking up as beams of sunlight began to penetrate between the branches of the big trees surrounding the camp buildings. Gil noticed that the kitchen was already alive with activity. Smoke arose from the fire in the ancient cook stove, and fragrant aromas, drifting from the dining hall stirred his appetite once more.

"What's on for today, Uncle Jim?" Jug asked twenty minutes later as he reached for one more pancake.

"Well, we need to get those trees cut around the dam before the water gets too high," he answered. "Some are big enough to cut for lumber and the rest can be cut for firewood to heat the cabins in the winter. We just need to get them cut down and dragged up the hill for now."

"Will we need to get a fire going in the tractor?" Gil asked. "We could pull the trees up the hill as soon as we get them cut."

The week before, they had found an old steam tractor in a tool shed, and although it was more than three quarters of a century old, it was in good shape. It only needed two things to make it run, water and firewood, and they had plenty of both. The only problem was, if you wanted to use the tractor, you had to plan ahead. The boiler had to be full of water and a roaring fire had to be started in the firebox to turn the water into steam. Once the water was hot, they would have power to spare.

"Yes," Jim replied to Gil's question. "We'll need to get the tractor fired up."

"Hey, someone's driving in!" Jug interrupted. Jumping up he ran to the nearest window and peered out. "It's the sheriff. I wonder what he's doing out here?"

Uncle Jim smiled. "I talked to him yesterday. He said he would bring a friend of his out here who might be interested in buying the logs that we need to cut away from the millpond. Tell him we're in here."

"Good morning," Gil greeted the sheriff as he stepped inside. At first glance, he looked like a man you wouldn't want to tangle with, but his smile soon put you at ease. They had only been at the camp a week and a half, but the events of those few days had brought them into contact with the sheriff many times. He was not only a good sheriff, but he had become a good friend too.

Gil observed the sheriffs friend, a muscular man in his early forties dressed in faded overalls and a flannel shirt. He gave Gil a warm smile and introduced himself as Jack Hankins.

"You guys are just in time for breakfast," Aunt Mary called as she came from the kitchen with two plates and some silverware. She filled two cups with coffee and slid them across the table toward the visitors.

"Don't usually eat breakfast," the sheriff protested. "But it does smell good." He slid up to the table and started loading his plate, motioning for his friend to join him.

"Jack, is a logger," he told them. "He'll take a look at what you've got." He paused and turned toward the teens. "Say, by the way, have you guys run across any more crooks around here? The county's been pretty quiet since we rounded up those characters last week."

"Haven't run into any more crooks," Gil answered.

"But we have come up with something of a mystery. Did you ever hear of a Superior Logging Company, or a Joe Green?"

A frown came to the sheriff's brow as he searched his memory. "No, can't say that I have," he answered. "How about you, Jack?"

"I've heard the old timers talk of Superior Logging, but

that was long before my time. Maybe some of the old fellows in town could help you. Guess I've never heard of Joe Green."

"Say, before I forget," the sheriff changed the subject. "I've got an old friend coming to visit me later this week. Would you mind if I brought my boat out here and parked it for a few days? He loves to fish and from what you boys tell me, this lake would be a good place to take him."

"Sure, you're welcome to park it in here," Uncle Jim nodded his head. "We'll keep an eye on it."

"Hey Gil," Jug spoke softly. "We'd better go get the fire started in the tractor soon or it won't be ready when we need it."

"Good idea," Gil replied, and they headed outside while the men finished their breakfast.

A few minutes later, with a fire roaring in the firebox of the tractor, Gil commented, "That should hold it for a while, let's go get the chainsaws and see where the men went."

Gil opened the door of the generator building. "I'll get the chainsaws, if you want to bring the gas and oil." They gathered up the equipment and headed around the building toward the pond. "Look how much the water has raised," Jug called.

"It sure has," Gil replied. "It's almost up to those smaller trees over there." Across the pond, Jack the logger was marking some of the bigger trees with a can of spray paint. Those trees would be saved to cut into lumber, and the rest would be cut for firewood.

"Well, we'd better start cutting," Jug spoke up stepping up to a couple of small maples. "I'll start with these two here."

"Ok," Gil agreed. "I'll move over a little so we don't get in each other's way." He moved to a six inch birch tree a hundred feet away and started his saw. The tree leaned over the water and he thought to himself: *I'll have to fall the top in the water. As long as the trunk is on dry ground, we can pull it out in a few minutes.* Touching the saw to the tree, he soon had it and several others laying on the ground. Laying the saw down, he called, "I'm going to check on the tractor."

At the tractor, he filled the firebox again, then went around to the side of the boiler where he carefully touched it. *It's lukewarm already,* he observed. *Another forty five minutes and it should be ready to go.*

When he returned to the pond, the visitors had already left and Uncle Jim was cutting a large tree with the saw he had been using. "Fire's going good," he reported. "Probable be ready in another forty five minutes."

Then he turned and called to Jug, "Want me to give you a break?"

Over the next hour the woods was a noisy place as chainsaws roared, tree trunks cracked and popped then splashed in the pond, or thumped as they hit the ground.

Later, when it was Gil's turn for a break, he told them, "I'm going to go check the tractor." He headed into the trees and as he drew near to the tractor, he could hear steam escaping from the pressure relief valve. "Good," he said. "Steam's up, and we're ready to go!"

He could feel the heat radiating from the boiler as he stepped up on the tractor and sat down. Steam pressure was at 180 pounds. Reaching for a rope, he gave it a tug and the ear piercing "toot" of the whistle sounded through trees.

With his hand around the throttle lever, he carefully pushed it, and the old tractor began to move as big chugs of steam and smoke puffed from the stack. He grabbed the steering wheel with both hands, swinging the tractor around in a big circle toward an opening in the trees..

"Hey Gil, wait for us," a voice yelled from the dining room door. Lori and Ann wanted a ride.

He waited for them to catch up, then headed into the woods at the breathtaking speed of three miles per hour.

As they neared the pond, the girls jumped off, and Gil backed the tractor up to a fallen tree. He jumped down and loosened one end of a chain fastened to the tractor. "We'll hook these tongs to the tree trunk, and I'll pull it up the hill," he told the girls.

As he inched the tractor forward to tighten the chain, the points of the tongs pulled into the wood, and the old tractor chugged and puffed smoke and steam high overhead. Gil opened the throttle further. But the tree was no match for it's power, and moments later it lay high up on the hill among the maples, waiting to be cut and trimmed at a later date.

The little clearing around the pond began to grow bigger as tree after tree was cut and pulled to the hilltop. Finally, about eleven o'clock, Uncle Jim called, "That's the last of them," he pointed to a couple of trees laying on the ground. "The rest of them will be above the water line. When you're done, take the tractor back where you got it."

Soon Gil backed up to the last tree. The sprawling top of the giant maple had fallen into the pond and the trunk lay between two large stumps only five feet apart. Gil watched carefully as he inched the tractor forward and the tree began to move. "Don't stand too close," he warned the others. "When it begins to bind between those two stumps, something's going to give!"

The almost branchless tree trunk slid along easily for the first forty feet and as the spreading treetop began to bind between the stumps, Gil opened the throttle.

Something was going to bind and something was going to have to break if the tree was going to slide between the trees.

Suddenly, forward movement slowed to a snail's pace and the old tractor chugged with all it's might. "Come on old girl," Gil called. "You can do it." Every powerful chug of the engine shook the air in the clearing as the tree inched on. Smaller branches began to pop and crack from the great force. Then with a bang as loud as a deer rifle, a large branch broke and the treetop slid clear of the stumps. The old steamer had won the battle, and moments later the tree lay at the top of the hill. Gil called, "Let's grab the tools and we'll head in for lunch." Quickly, Jug and Ann grabbed the tools and headed off through the trees.

Lori stepped up on the tractor and said, "I'll ride back with you." As the tractor headed into the trees, she glanced back at the pond and said, "Look, the water is already coming up around some of the stumps that you cut this morning."

Looking over his shoulder, Gil replied. "I guess I was too busy to notice. But I wouldn't be surprised if the water is going to be high enough to try the generator tonight."

"We've got to go to town to get some electrical supplies," Jim announced as they were eating lunch. "If the generator works, we may as well have lights ready, and if it doesn't, we'll still need them soon, we'll just have to have a different generator. You guys can go along if you'd like to."

"Maybe we could take the glass jar to town and have the sheriff keep it for us," Gil suggested. "That way it would be safe until we decide what to do with it."

"Good idea," Jim agreed. "Get your things around and we'll leave just as soon as you're ready"

An hour later, Gil's eyes swept over the town in the valley below. It was not large, just a grocery store, a hardware, post office, and a handful of small businesses. The sheriff shared his office with the other county officials in the center of town. *It's small, but it has a character of it's own, he thought. Like it's part of the family.*

Uncle Jim dropped the ladies off at the grocery store and then parked in front of the hardware.

"I'm going to see the sheriff," Gil told him. He picked up a brown paper bag from the back of the pickup that contained the old jar and turned toward the sheriff's office.

"I'm coming with you," Jug spoke up.

"I'll be in the hardware," Jim explained. "We'll pick up Mary and the girls at the grocery store when we're done."

Moments later Gil and Jug stood in the sheriffs office. "What can I do for you?" the receptionist asked.

"We'd like to see the sheriff he's not too busy," Gil told her.

"Let me check." She spoke into her phone, then said, "He'll be right with you."

Seconds later the sheriff's door opened and he called, "Come on in boys."

"What ya got, a bag of fish for me?"

"No," Gil laughed. "We found this in the lake yesterday and wondered if you'd keep it for us?" He lifted the jar and plastic dish of coins from the bag and set it in front of the sheriff. "It was in about eight feet of water and fifty feet off shore," he added, popping the lid off the dish to expose the contents.

A look of surprise crossed the sheriff's face as he examined the things. "It appears to have been in the water for a long time, from your description." Checking the watch and locket with a magnifying glass, he asked, "That's why you wanted to know about Joe Green?"

"Yes," Gil responded.

"Well, it looks like you've found yourself a fine treasure," he smiled and carefully placed the things back in the plastic dish. "I can put this where it's safe if you'd like me to. Other than those crooks we took care of last week, nobody I know of has been on that lake for years. It'll be almost impossible to trace this stuff after such a long time."

"If you don't mind, we'll leave it with you for now," Gil told him. "We really appreciate your help."

"No problem," the sheriff replied. "Say, by the way. Sometimes about this time of day, there's a couple of old timers that sit on the bench in front of the hardware store talking. You might ask them about this Joe Green. They used to be loggers, so if anyone would remember him, they would be the ones."

"Thanks again," Gil replied as they headed out the door.

Approaching the hardware, Gil was disappointed that the bench in front was empty. "Oh well. Let's go inside and see if we can help Uncle Jim."

"Hey boys, you're just in time to help carry these supplies to the truck," Uncle Jim called from the counter where he was checking out his purchases.

"I'll get this electric wire," Gil scooped up the rolls and headed for the truck. Setting them down, he turned to check on Jug.

"I need a hand!" Jug called, his arms loaded to capacity. "Uncle Jim said he could get the rest of the things."

Gil began to stack the supplies in the back of the truck. By the time they got groceries, electrical supplies, and four teens in the back of the pickup, it would be full.

He had just reached for the last box when Jug said softly, "Don't look now, but there's a couple of old fellows heading this way."

Gil sneaked a quick look. One man was thin and tall while the other was short and heavy set. Both had snow white hair. The taller was clean shaven, but the shorter man's face was covered with a full beard. They were talking as they moved closer and paused by the bench.

Suddenly the short man sneezed and quickly reached into his pocket. Withdrawing his handkerchief, several coins came along with it and fell to the sidewalk, then rolled off the curb and landed at the boy's feet.

Gil bent over and gathered up the coins. Straightening up, he held out his hand and spoke to the man, "Here's the change you dropped."

"Thank you, thank you," the man responded. "That's my coffee money," he explained. "Just can't remember not to put it in my pocket with my handkerchief." He took the coins and stuffed them right back in the same pocket, then asked, "You from 'round here?"

"Not really, Gil answered. "My uncle just bought an old logging camp about ten miles south of here. That's where we're staying."

"Logging camp? Ten miles south?" He hesitated like he was in deep thought. Then suddenly his eyes brightened and he looked up. "The old Superior Sawmill? By the lake?"

"It's by a lake," Jug spoke up. "You say it was the Superior Sawmill?"

"Been so many years ago, I'd almost forgotten. But that's what they called her," he answered.

"Did you ever hear of a man called Joe Green?" Gil questioned.

The man grew silent, then leaned against the back of the bench, and his hand went to his forehead like a student trying to remember the answer to the questions on a test. "Green, Green?" the old man mumbled.

Suddenly, the taller man turned to his friend and asked, "Wasn't that the woods boss' name when we were working at the logging camp?"

A scowl crossed his brow. "Woods boss? Can't remember. A tall guy? You mean that tall guy named Joe--- Joe, yes, Joe Green! That was his name."

All at once the tall fellow became very serious. "Why you ask 'bout Joe Green? How ya know 'im?"

Gil's mind raced. He didn't want to scare the old fellow off, yet at the same time, he didn't want to give out too many details either. "Oh, we found something at the camp with his name on it. We were just wondering who he was and if he's still around? The sheriff said you fellows would probably know him if anyone would, so that's why we're asking."

His reply seemed to set them at ease and they sat down on the bench. "He was a little older than Slim and me. Haven't seen him in probably fifty years. You seen him Slim?"

"Nope," he looked down and stared at the sidewalk. "Lived in a lit'l town south of the camp. Railroad ran thru then. Lot's a lit'l bergs long the tracks, those days. They jus went away when they took the tracks up."

"You mean there was a little town south of the logging camp?" Gil questioned the men.

"Used to be," the short fellow answered. Probably all rotted down by now," he concluded.

Out the corner of his eye, Gil saw his uncle come out of the hardware and walk toward them "I'd like you to meet my Uncle Jim," he told the men as Jim stepped up beside them. "And thanks so much for the information you gave us. We've got to get going now. The ladies are over grocery shopping, and we can't keep the cooks waiting too long."

Climbing into the truck, he thought, *We've probably learned all we 're going to from the old men. But at least, now we know where to start.*

Jim drove the truck to the grocery store and Gil spoke up, "Want me to go find the girls?"

"Sure," Jim replied. "We'll stay here with the truck." Entering the store, Gil spotted the girls checking out. "I'll wheel one of those carts for you," he offered and a few minutes later they were loaded into the old truck and heading out of town.

Riding in the back on a cushion, Lori asked, "Did you learn anything from the sheriff?"

Gil replied, "He said he didn't think there was any way we could figure out how the things got in the lake. It's just been too long. Still, I don't feel right about keeping it and not trying to find out who it belonged to."

"Yes," Lori agreed. "It had to be lost a long time ago. My dad's found a lot of old things with his metal detector, and from what he's learned about lost things, I think you have every right to keep it. But it does make you wonder why it was in the lake. Every time I think about it, I see the face in that locket and wonder, who was she, and why was her picture with Joe Green's things."

"I know," Gil agreed. "I'm tempted to just forget about

looking any farther. But then I keep remembering a gold ring that Grandma gave me for my tenth birthday. I really thought a lot of that ring. Then one day I lost it on the ball field at school, and a couple of months later I saw one of the big kids wearing it on his little finger. I tried to tell him that it was mine, but he just laughed and said, *That's tough, kid It's mine now!*"

"Yes, I see what you mean," Lori gave him an understanding smile.

Lori always seemed to understand, he took her hand and gave it a squeeze. Soon his thoughts turned to Joe Green. *What did Slim say about a little town just to the south of the camp? But the county map didn't show anything near the logging camp. Hey, wait a minute, he remembered. The sheriff gave us a stack of old maps. Would the older ones show a town nearby? Could there have been a town close to the camp?*

CHAPTER IV
LIGHTS

I t was three o'clock when they pulled up in front of the dining hall. "Let's help unload the groceries," Uncle Jim told them. "Then we'll get some electric wires strung between the buildings."

The opening in the forest soon became alive with activity. "Let's get this roll of heavy wire strung up between the kitchen and the generator first," Jim directed. "Then we'll work on lights.

"Ok," Gil replied uncoiling a couple of loops of wire.

"There, that should be enough to get into the building. Now if one of you girls would stand on the end of it, Jug and I will roll the rest out to the generator building. Then we'll come back and hang it up in the air so it'll be out of the way."

The roll was heavy and hard to handle, but with each revolution it became easier to control. Looking back, Jug asked, "Are we going straight toward the barn?"

"I think so," Gil replied. "If we follow the path we've been using, we'll be in pretty good shape, that is if we have enough wire."

"Don't talk like that," Jug scolded, and a couple of minutes later he noted, "Oh good, we have plenty of wire. What do we do next?"

"Uncle Jim is putting a breaker box in the kitchen, so let's go back and start hanging the wire there." Gil answered.

Back at the kitchen Uncle Jim already had the wire anchored to an insulator up on the side of the building. "You'll have to hang it on trees the rest of the way," he directed. "I'll need Jug here. The girls can give you a hand."

"We'll try to fasten it to that tree," Gil pointed to it. "Bring that bag of insulators and I'll carry this ladder over there."

Setting the ladder against the tree, Gil headed up with an insulator and a screwdriver. With the screwdriver stuck through the hole in the insulator he quickly turned the screw end of it firmly into the tree.

Stepping back to the ground, he said to the girls, "Pick the wire up and set it on my shoulder. That way both of my hands will be :free." Carefully climbing the ladder he hooked the wire over the insulator and fastened it in place with a piece of wire.

Back on the ground, he looked up at the wire, "That looks good. Let's fasten it to that next tree over there."

Over the next hour, they repeated the process several times until the wire had been raised in the air all the way to the generator barn. Pausing to look at his watch, Gil said, "That's not bad time. Let's go check with the others."

"How's it going?" Ann called as they approached the kitchen.

"Another half hour and we'll be all set on this end," her father answered. "Gil, would you give us a hand here? I think we can have it all set for lights on this end by the time supper is ready. After we eat, we should have time to get it hooked to the generator, then we'll see if we have power."

Later as they bowed their heads to give thanks, Gil prayed, "Thank you Lord for this food, and we pray that the generator would work for us - - ."

Waiting for Jug to fix his hamburger so he would pass the platter on, Gil nudged Lori to get her attention. Nodding his head slightly toward Jug, they watched.

"Can you believe that," he whispered softly. First Jug took a burger from the platter, grabbed a bun and buttered it, then put mustard, catsup, and salad dressing on top followed by a slice of cheese, chip dip, and finally the burger. But that wasn't the end. On top of the burger, a slice of tomato, lettuce, and dill pickles were followed by another slice of cheese, catsup, mustard, and salad dressing. And of course, the top half of the bun. Finally finished, he squashed it down so he could get his mouth over it and took a big bite.

"Boy, I sure do like your hamburgers Mrs. West," he called.

"How do you know what a hamburger tastes like?" Gil questioned. "With all that junk you put on it, I don't know how you could ever taste that little piece of meat you put in there!"

"You're just jealous of my sandwich making abilities," Jug boasted between bites.

Later, when everyone had finished eating, Uncle Jim told them, "We have to finish hooking up the wires to the generator, so we'd better get started before it gets dark. Girls, when you're done helping Mary clean up the tables, there are a couple of electric cords and some clamp on lights over there. By the time you get them set up in here, we'll be ready to try the generator."

Gil tightened the last screw an hour and a half later and asked, "I think that about finishes it, doesn't it?" Voices outside told him the girls had finished their job and had come to join them.

Taking a quick glance around him, Jim answered, "Yes, I think so. Let's go check the water."

From the doorway Jug called, "Beat ya to the dam," and took off out the door as fast as he could run.

Caught off guard, Gil dropped his screwdriver and leaped through the door. "He won't beat me," he promised Lori as his long legs carried him toward the dam.

"Better not miss this," Lori told Ann and hurried to catch up with the fellows.

It was a friendly rivalry, but Gil put everything he had into the race. He knew Jug couldn't outrun him, and Jug knew it too, that is, *unless* he had a head start.

Poor Jug, he just wasn't built for a race, with short legs, and after eating three of his burger specials, he was carrying just a little extra weight. He struggled through some low growing brush, then headed on as fast as he could go.

Just behind, Gil cleared the same clump of brush with a great leap, which closed much of the gap between the two boys. At the comer of the building, he was just one step behind Jug.

With just a few feet yet to go, and realizing he didn't have a big enough head start, Jug turned and tackled Gil as he tried to pass. He couldn't win in a foot race, but he had the upper hand when it came to a tackle.

The two boys went rolling across the ground. Suddenly, Gil untangled himself and leaped to his feet.

"I hear water running!" Looking around, he cried out. "Hey, look, the dam is full, and the water wheel is turning!"

Jug scrambled to his feet and brushed himself off. "That's great news," he yelled.

"But if the water wheel is turning, why don't we have lights?" Ann questioned.

"Isn't it going to work?" Lori stepped up beside Gil, her voice showing disappointment.

A smile crossed Gil's face. "The belt inside isn't hooked up to the generator yet." he explained. "If it was hooked directly to the generator and something went wrong, we'd have to drain the dam in order to work on it. Let's go inside and I'll show you."

"The dam's full and the water wheel is running," Jug called to Uncle Jim who was coming through the trees toward them.

"Great," Jim responded. "I think everything is ready inside. Let's get it going."

Moving over by the generator, Gil pointed to a foot wide pulley on the shaft heading out to the waterwheel. A belt on that pulley was spinning one half of a double pulley attached to the generator, but the generator was not turning. "We just have to force this turning belt over on to the other half of the pulley, to get the generator to run," he explained.

Jim reached out to a long lever. As he moved the lever, it began to push the turning belt onto the generator pulley. It slipped on the generator at first, then slowly it began to turn. As he applied more pressure to the belt, suddenly with a couple of screeches, the generator reved up to full speed.

"But we still don't have any lights," Ann moaned.

"What do we do now," Lori asked. Then a split second later, her eyebrows raised, and she reached out and flipped a switch beside her. Instantly the room was filled with light. "I guess it does help if you turn the switch on,' 'she giggled.

"Hey, we made it work," Jim spoke up. "Good job guys." He bent down to check the oil in two little cups that kept the bearings oiled. "We have to keep oil in these, or we'll be in the dark again. Well, I guess everything here is ok for now, let's go see if Mary has any light!"

As they moved out of the trees, Jug pointed toward the kitchen window. "Either Aunt Mary lit a lantern, or the lights are working!"

"It looks pretty bright for a lantern," Gil observed.

Aunt Mary greeted them as they stepped into the dining room. "Oh, thank you! Cooking is going to be a lot easier soon," she predicted, setting a big plate of chocolate chip cookies on the table. "That old wood cook stove does warm things up in the summertime," she said wiping the sweat from her brow.

"By the way, did you fellows find out anything about Joe Green while you were in town today?" she inquired.

Gil replied, "The sheriff didn't know, but he told us about a couple of old fellows who might know something, and later we got to talk to them for a couple of minutes."

"Did they know anything?

"They told us that this place used to be the Superior Sawmill, and that Joe Green was their boss at the time," Gil began to fill her in on the details. The strange thing was, they said he lived in a little town just south of here."

"But there aren't any towns close to the camp," Jim said firmly. "Before we bought this camp, we flew over this area. They said the nearest town was ten miles away. To the south, there's just the woods, the river and swamps.

"That's what I thought," Gil replied. "But the two old timers told us that there were a lot of little settlements along the railroad tracks, before they took the tracks out. When the mill and the mine closed, there weren't any jobs left, so the people went other places to get work. They said the town had probably fallen down and rotted away by now."

"Do you suppose we could find anything on those county maps the sheriff gave us last week?" Jug asked, then jumped up and ran to the kitchen. Returning, he laid a stack of maps on the table and the four teens gathered around them.

Lori picked up the top map and said, "This is last years map. We'd better dig deeper in the pile."

Lifting the comers of the maps, Gil pulled one from the pile and studied it for a moment. "This is twenty years old, but nothing much has changed."

They dug deeper in the pile and Jug spread another map out in front of him. "This one shows an unimproved trail in to the camp."

Gil leaned closer and studied the map for a moment. He pointed to a line and said, "I wonder what this line is? See, it comes from the direction of town, then goes through this camp and around the south side of the lake, and then heads off to the west."

Sitting close to Gil, Lori studied the map legend carefully and announced, "This shows that it would be an abandoned railroad."

Gil nodded in agreement. "Let's get these newer maps out of the way," he told them. Picking up three quarters of the pile, he lay them out of the way on a nearby table. "There, now let's see what we have."

Studying the map on the top of the pile, he spoke, "This is more like it," he pointed to a clearly marked railroad.

"Yes, here's our camp," Lori pointed. "It says Superior Sawmill."

"Must be the copper mine was still operating on the other side of the lake," Jug concluded.

Gil's eyes slowly swept over the map. *There's a lot of trails here, but they all seem to lead back to the railroad, he thought. This railroad branch heads to the abandoned mine and meets with the main tracks south of the lake. But I just don't see a town. Am I missing something?*

"There's a smudge or something here," Gil started to speak. "I wonder - -?"

Lori picked up a pencil and started to rub the eraser gently on the spot. A few strokes is all it took to erase most of the spot. "Look, there's a dot there beside the railroad. Does that mark a town?"

Gil raised the map to catch the light better. "D-A-NE-S. Danes?" *The letters are so faded thay're hard to make out*, he thought. D-A-N-E-S-V---E." He moved the map slightly. "V-I-L-L-E," he read the letters.

"Danesville?" Lori questioned. "Do you think that's the town?"

"I don't know," Gil replied. "But there's nothing else. That must be it."

"Hey you guys, do you know what time it is?" Uncle Jim interrupted. "We'd better get things wrapped up and hit the sack." Picking up his Bible, he opened it to Luke 12, and read, *"The ground of a certain rich man produced abundant crops. So he said to himself, I will build bigger barns, - - - there will I store all my fruit, --- I will say to my soul, I have many goods laid up for many years; I will take it easy, --- I will eat, drink and be merry."* Pausing for a moment, Jim explained, "The rich man made great plans. He thought he had everything under control. But he had forgotten God and completely left him out of his plans. God had given him health, strength, and riches, but he gave God no place in his life at all."

"Then suddenly, in the middle of all his planning, God said," *"Thou fool, this night you are going to die! Then who is going to possess all that you have gained?"*

Solomon tells us in Proverbs, *"Trust in the Lord with all your heart; and lean not to your own understanding. In all your ways acknowledge Him, and he shall direct your paths."* Uncle Jim closed his Bible and said, God is so wise and powerful that he created this great universe that we live in. He's so intelligent that he controls everything at once and keeps it in proper orbit. Even though he is busy doing these things, God still loves us and wants to help us with every step we take. He wants every step to be in the right direction so we don't fall and get hurt and waste the precious time and resources that he has given us."

Heading for the bunkhouses, Lori stopped to take in the beauty of the campgrounds, and Gil stepped up beside her. "Isn't it beautiful?" she said softly. Their eyes swept over their surroundings. Stars twinkled like tiny beacons, and the moon that was beginning to settle into the western sky, turned the lake into a shimmering pool of sparkling diamonds.

"Yes, it's so peaceful here," Gil responded.

"You know Gil, when I decided to come up here for the summer, I was only thinking of what a fun time it would be. I thought it would be nice to get away from my mom and little sisters yelling at me all the time. It seems like I have so little time to call my own. Life just seemed so busy, so confusing, like a mad cycle without any purpose or direction. I've been a Christian since I was five, so I realized God was out there somewhere, even that he was in my heart, but he seemed so far away from me in my everyday life. But God just seems to be so much closer up here. I feel like I can reach out and touch Him."

Gil took her hand in his. "Yes, I know what you mean," he replied. Lori was the oldest of the children in her family, and her father had to be out of town a lot, sometimes for a month at a time. With her parents and younger sisters in a small house, Gil could understand her feeling of being overwhelmed and in a mad rush of confusion. Lori was very special to him and he had sensed that she had been having a struggle with the situation at home.

"I love my mom and sisters," Lori continued. "But I do need to take a serious look at my own future, too."

"I know how you feel," Gil squeezed her hand. "When I see this abandoned camp here in the woods, and then discover there once was a town nearby where people lived and worked and made plans for the future, and now they tell us that it' s probably all fallen down and rotted into the ground, I wonder.

Did those people include God in their plans? Or did they just live and then fade into the past without a memory?"

Lori tightened her grip on his hand and said, "Yes. God certainly must have meant for life to be more than that."

Later as Gil crawled into his bunk for the night, he asked God to help him with the decisions he would soon have to make about his own future. "And be with Lori," he prayed. "Help her at this time that she would make the right choices."

Gil's mind had not slowed down enough to sleep. Questions kept coming back, again and again. *Joe Green couldn't still be alive, could he? No, that's asking too much*, his mind concluded. *Besides, how could an old person like that survive in the wilderness without even a road to bring in supplies to his house? He hadn't been seen around in many years. No, he can't still be alive. But it would be interesting to explore a real ghost town to see what's left of it, if anything is.*

CHAPTER V
EXPLORING

"ey, you going to sleep all day?" Jug's voice called sounding very far away.

Gil stirred slightly in his bunk.

"Ok, just go ahead and sleep." Jugs voice was much closer now. "I wont have to share breakfast with you. Maybe I can get my fair share this morning."

Suddenly, Gil was wide awake. He wasn't in the woods, he was still in his bunk, and Jug was already dressed and thinking about breakfast. He had to get up fast and get to the dining hall before Jug ate all the food. He jumped out of bed and quickly dressed then stepped outside.

"We're going to have to go fishing one of these nights soon," Jug called from the spring. "Fish are really jumping. Some big ones."

"First chance we get," Gil agreed. The sound of a bunkhouse door closing caught Gil's attention and he turned to see Uncle Jim and Aunt Mary heading for the kitchen.

When breakfast was done, Gil slid back from the table and asked, "What's on for the day?" "I want to get some permanent lights in this building and in the bunkhouses." Jim replied. "This afternoon, I plan to go to town and pick up a new refrigerator and stove and some pipe to drive a well. When we get hooked up with running water, I'm going to get a crew from our church to help us with some of the bigger projects that we have to do."

A few minutes later the building was alive with activity. Gil used a saw to cut holes for wall plugs and lights, while Jug and Uncle Jim ran wires between the holes.

"We'd better get the wires run in the attic before the sun gets on the roof," Gil warned. "Otherwise it'll get too hot to work up there."

It was almost noon when Gil called to his uncle, "We need six more wall plugs and a ceiling light for each of the bunk houses."

Pulling a pad from his shirt pocket, Jim added the things to his list. "I'll pick them up in town this afternoon. Is there anything else we need?"

"I could use a gallon of chocolate cherry ice cream!" Jug called from the other side of the room.

"I'll be glad to bring you some, if the hardware has it in stock," Uncle Jim smiled. "Ok, I think Mary has some sandwiches ready for us. Let's get cleaned up so we can eat."

"What do you have for us to do this afternoon?" Gil inquired.

"Well, we made better progress this morning than I thought we might," Jim replied sitting down to the table. "If you want to take the afternoon off, we can finish with the electrical hookups after supper tonight."

Moments later, Jug leaned over and spoke to Gil as they ate. "I'd like to go fishing, but it's the wrong time of the day for the fish to bite. What are you thinking?"

"I've been thinking," Gil responded. "It might be fun to find that old town on the other side of the lake."

"Yes, that sound's kind of exciting," Jug answered.

"But how are we going to find it way out there in the middle of the woods?"

Gil reached for a map from the far end of the table and spread it out in front of them. "The way I see it, we canoe across the lake and down the creek running out of the south end of the lake. About a half mile down the creek, we should run across the old railroad grade. At that point the railroad should be running almost due west toward the old town."

Jug's eyes brightened. "I think you're right. We shouldn't get lost, with the river to the south and east of us, and the lake on the north. Besides, the old town was on the railroad. We should be able to follow it to the town and back."

"What are you guys plotting?" Ann interrupted.

"Are we included?" Lori questioned.

"Well now," Jug replied. "Good cooks are always welcome in our plans!"

"Just talking about a little exploring," Gil explained his plan to them. "Let's see what Uncle Jim thinks."

Uncle Jim sat in silence for a moment studying the map. "Looks like a pretty good plan. But with every good plan, you need to allow for a margin of error. This is a very remote area and you can't take any chances. You'll need your compasses, and you must depend on them, not on your hunches. A couple of you ought to take a waterproof box of matches with you. If the temperature drops and you get lost, you can build a fire to stay warm. I know I don't have to tell Jug this, but take some snacks with you. There's a roll of flame orange survey ribbon on the shelf in the kitchen. Use that to mark the trail so you can find your way back without any trouble."

"Can we go too, Dad?" Ann interrupted.

"I don't see any reason why you can't if you want to," he replied. "Just don't take any chances. That old jar and the things in it aren't worth any one of you getting hurt. I plan to be back about five o'clock, and I'll need some help to unload the heavy things," he explained.

"Ok, Uncle Jim. We'll be careful." Gil responded.

"We won't take any unnecessary chances." Quickly, he stood and started to clean up the tables. "Let's hurry so we'll have plenty of time to explore."

Ten minutes later they gathered by the canoes and checked their things. "I've got my compass, matches and food," Jug told them.

"How about you girls?" Gil asked.

"We're all set," they responded.

Reaching into the large pockets of a vest he wore, Gil checked his supplies. "Matches, snacks, survey ribbon, knife, map, water," he checked off his list. "And I've got some bug repellant, and a small first aid kit, just in case someone needs it."

"Sounds like we're all set," Jug reasoned. "Let's get the show on the road." He reached out and untied the canoe and gave it a push into the water.

"Get in the back, Jug," Gil called out. "Then you girls get in and I'll shove us off."

Slipping off his shoes, he laid them in the canoe and pushed it out into deeper water, then jumped in and settled down in the front. His weight pushed the canoe to the bottom momentarily, but then the canoe stabilized itself and floated free.

Gil grabbed a paddle and pushed the front around toward the south shore. "Ok, let's go."

Four paddles dug deep into the water and the canoe began to shoot forward. "See that little notch in the trees over there," Jug pointed. "That's where the creek is, so let's head for it." From the back of the canoe he kept them lined up with their destination on the opposite shore.

To Gil, the trees didn't seem to be getting any closer for several minutes, but then slowly they began to inch closer. Dip and pull, dip and pull, they drove the canoe on at a steady pace and soon the trees along the shore began to move quickly toward them.

"I can't see where the creek is in all those cattails," Jug called.

"It's to the left," Gil yelled back. Then a moment later, he called out, "Hard to the right!" and the canoe slipped silently between the cattails into the creek.

A six foot high wall of cattails blocked their vision for the first two hundred feet and there was little current to help them along. Soon evergreens began to take over the banks and they moved into higher ground where hardwood trees rose up high and spread over the creek.

"Tree down in the creek ahead," Gil warned. "Swing to the left." He pulled his end over and they squeezed through the opening," Jug noted as the stream narrowed and the canoe gained speed.

"Hold her down, there's a sharp bend to the right," Gil told them. "Let's keep to the inside of the curve." and he pulled the front in close. The fast flowing current on the outside of the bend could be a problem if they got crossways of to the current, and one thing they didn't want to do was to capsize in this cold water.

Just beyond the bend, low hanging branches distracted them for a moment and looking ahead, Gil yelled out, "Rapids ahead. Watch out for the rocks. Keep it straight in the center of the creek," he yelled like a ship's captain barking out orders.

To stay out of trouble canoeing, there wasn't always time to be polite. Being too slow or not knowing what the others were going to do could mean a cold bath for everyone.

For the next quarter mile, the stream wandered back and forth through the big trees. As they rounded another bend, Ann glanced up and cried out, "What happened to the creek!"

Gil looked up quickly and saw what she meant. The stream seemed to disappear into the brush. "Let's ease over to the right into the still water," he instructed. "We'd better take a closer look."

"It's a big tree that's blown down across the creek," Jug commented. "Do you think we can squeeze through on the other side?"

"Maybe. But let's try to back up the creek a little so we don't get crossways," Gil suggested, and they quickly worked themselves backwards upstream until they had room to maneuver.

"It looks like there might be room enough to get through," Gil suggested. "Let's hit it!"

They dug their paddles deep and shot quickly across the creek. Their momentum quickly carried them through the brush to the other side, where they found a large pool of deep still water.

Pausing to rest a minute at the pool, Jug asked, "Shouldn't we be getting close to the old railroad?"

"It seems like it," Gil replied. He was about to say, "Let's push on," when something caught his eye. Something didn't look quite normal, and he motioned for them to pull into the right bank.

The stream was narrow with high banks where the tree had fallen across the creek, but just beyond, the banks dropped off quickly and a deep pool had formed.

"It looks like someone made a big pile of dirt on both sides of the creek there," Lori motioned.

"Yes, that's what caught my eye," Gil agreed. "It's not a nice round hill like the rest of them along the stream. It's got a flat spot on the top, and the sides are real steep, and why is there another hill just like it on the other side that lines up with this one?"

"Could the railroad have crossed here," Jug questioned. "That's a possibility," Gil nodded. "We'd better take a closer look. We sure don't want to have to paddle back upstream any more than we have to, just because we went farther than we had to."

Jug stepped out on the bank and held the canoe until the others had stepped out.

"Let's set it up on the bank so it doesn't get away," Gil suggested. "And we'd better tie it to that tree there, just to be safe."

With the canoe well secured, Gil turned toward the steep bank, pulled the brush back and began to work his way up the hill. The brush was thick and it was tough going, but by pushing and pulling he was making some progress. Then all at once, a tree trunk about a foot in diameter blocked his way. Moving to one side he discovered another the same size. He paused for a moment, thinking, *I don't remember any trees that size sticking out of this bank There couldn't have been. The flat top on this hill was clearly visible.*

Examining the trees more closely, he reached for his pocket knife, and opening the large blade, he stuck it into the wood and pried a small piece of it free. Suddenly, it began to make sense. *This isn't bark, he discovered. This is weathered wood.* Raising the chip to his nose, he smelled it. *The unmistakable odor of creosote!*

"Hey, guys! This is it. I found the posts that held up the railroad trestle."

"Great," Jug called from above him. "And I just found an easier way to get to the top."

Moments later, they all stood at the top of the bank, twelve feet above the creek. Looking to the west, Gil spoke. "Look there. The road bed is pretty obvious going into the trees and it's heading in the right direction too," he said checking his compass.

Gil pulled the old map from his pocket and unfolded it. "It shows the railroad heading almost straight west from here. Let's tie a piece of that orange ribbon on this tree so we can find our way back."

With the ribbon in place, Jug asked, "Are we ready to head down the trail? It's pretty easy to see where it goes from here."

"We're ready. Let's go." Gil told him and they started down the road bed.

"The way the trees arch out over the trail makes it look like we're going into a tunnel," Lori observed as they walked along.

The roadbed had been cut through several little hills which made it easy to follow. Thick leaves on the big trees overhead shut out so much light that the forest floor was almost bare of undergrowth. They made good time as they hurried along. They had traveled a hundred yards when Gil stopped and looked back. "You can still see that ribbon back there, but we have plenty of it, so let's put another one here."

"Good idea," Lori responded taking the ribbon Gil handed her, she tied it to a branch that overhung the trail. "We don't want to miss the trail coming back."

Moving on another hundred yards, the forest floor leveled out into a large flat area. Here the trail was not so easy to spot and Gil paused for a moment. Looking back down the trail behind them, he said. "We can still see ribbons that we put up behind us, but I can't spot the trail ahead for sure. Now, we know that railroad tracks can't make a ninety degree bend, and the map shows the tracks going pretty much west for several miles, so where did it go from this point?"

Jug thought a moment before replying, "If we assume the trail goes on west, one of us can go on ahead a little. If we keep putting up a ribbon every little ways that lines up those back there, then we can find our way back safely, if we don't pick up the trail ahead."

"Right," Gil replied. "That's about what I was thinking. Want to try it?"

"Sure," the others agreed.

Gil stepped to the right a little to line up with the trail behind them and tied up another ribbon. "Ok, Jug, if you would go back to the last ribbon, you can keep me lined up with this one, and I'll move on a little to see what we can find."

"Ok," Jug responded and took off back down the trail.

"Don't go too far," Lori warned Gil as he moved into the trees.

"I won't," he answered and moved on a hundred feet, then stopped to look back. *I can still see Jug, but I need to move to the left a couple of steps,* he thought. Looking around, he saw no signs of the railroad bed, so he tied up another ribbon and moved another fifty paces to the west.

Stopping again, he looked back. *Jug is almost out of sight,* he observed. *Time to tie up another ribbon,* and he motioned for Jug to come forward a little. The ribbons were doing their job. They marked the trail clearly back to the creek. Gil slowly swung around and let his eyes sweep over the forest floor. Ahead and to the right, there appeared to be several shallow holes in the ground. Although they didn't appear natural, they didn't quite line up with where he thought the trail should be. Still, there was no other sign of the roadbed.

As Gil turned to see if Jug had reached the next ribbon, his toe bumped something in the leaves. Distracted for a moment, he thought, *That doesn't feel like a piece of wood. It's too heavy.* Bending down, he picked it from the leaves.

"Wow. A railroad spike!" he cried and his brows raised high. "Hey you guys. Come on over here!" He motioned to them.

"What did you find?" Lori cried as she drew near.

Gil handed the spike to her. "The tracks had to be right in here somewhere." He pulled the map from his pocket and studied it for a moment. "Maybe that's the problem."

"What's that?" Lori questioned stepping up close to Gil. "See, the railroad splits here. One line goes up the west side of the lake towards the old copper mine, and the main line goes around the east side of the lake up to the logging camp."

"Do you think this is where the line splits off to go to the west side?" Lori asked.

"See those holes over there," he pointed. "Picture the main track going to the left of them, and on the right a track swings off to the north towards the mine."

"Yes, that makes sense," Lori agreed. "What should we do now?"

"You stay here where I can see you, and I'll take a circle off to the right, and then move around to the west a hundred feet or so and try to pick up the trail. Jug and Ann should be caught up to us by that time."

Moving to the north about thirty paces, Gil began to circle around to the west. He saw nothing until he had moved a hundred feet. There the ground began to drop off and he discovered several holes ahead about ten feet apart. He paused to get his bearings and looked back toward Lori. *Yes, they do line up in a big curve, he concluded. Now to circle back and see if I can find the main track*

Gil picked out a spot where he would come out ahead of Lori and started walking. As he moved on, the floor of the forest turned to little hills and hallows, and suddenly there before him, was clear evidence of the railroad bed again. We were right. The road did split here.

"Thank you Lord," he breathed a sigh of relief and motioned for the others to catch up. "Tie a ribbon on that tree just ahead when you go by," he called.

Together, on the trail once more, Gil checked his watch. "It's two o'clock now. If we're going to be back by five, we only have about an hour to search." Checking the map again, he suggested, "We should be getting close to where the town was."

"Ok, let's hit the trail," Jug spoke up and took off to the west at a fast pace.

The trail was much easier to follow now, and except for stopping to mark the trail, they pushed on for ten minutes. Suddenly, Ann stopped in her tracks. "Is that a gravestone there by that tree?" she pointed.

"Kind of looks like it," Jug replied stopping to look around. "Hey, there's another one over there."

Gil stepped to the closest stone. "Harry Smith, born 6-11-1832, died 2-27-1898," he read. "We must be near the town. This must have been their cemetery!"

Pushing on, Jug soon called, "Something's in the trees on the right." Checking it out, they discovered what appeared to be the shell of an old barn. The roof was sagging and the walls leaned off at crazy angles.

"It's not worth exploring right now," Gil concluded.

"Let's go a little farther and see if there's anything else left of the town."

After walking a little farther, dark shadows began to appear in the trees up ahead and Lori reached out for Gil's hand. "Do you think those are houses?"

"It could be," Gil gave her hand a squeeze. "It sure gives you a funny feeling, like we're trespassing into the past."

As the four pressed on side by side, Jug pointed to a building with a high false front facing the roadbed and read the sign dangling from one corner, "Smith's General Store."

"Hey, over there, is the railroad station," Ann observed. "You can tell by the shape of it."

Several more buildings lined either side of the tracks as they came to what appeared to be a cross street. Gil checked his watch again. "Only got ten minutes before we have to start back. I'm going to check this side street to the left."

"We'll go along," Jug responded.

They had moved down the street a half block when a large house came into view. "Would you believe that," Gil spoke up. "That house is made of bricks. Someone must have been quite prosperous to build a house like that out in the woods."

Across the street a much smaller house caught Gil's attention. He couldn't explain it, but something was different about the house. *But it'll just have to wait for another day, he thought. We have to head back now.*

Returning quickly along the well marked trail, Gil questioned the others, "What did you think of it?"

"It gave me an eerie feeling," Ann responded.

Frank Austin

"Me too," Lori agreed. "It looked like they just picked up their clothes and forgot to come back."

"What about you Jug?"

"Can't explain it, after what they told us about the town being rotted down to the ground. Then seeing that old wreck of a Barn fallen down when we came in, I thought if we found anything, it would look like the barn. It's weird! Didn't they say that the railroad was pulled out fifty years ago?"

"I think they said fifty years, but it looks like the buildings must have had some repairs on them several times since then. The roofs weren't falling in, and the windows, either had glass in them or had been boarded up. It's very strange," Gil told them.

CHAPTER VI
DRIVING A WELL

ow! That's a bear going against the current!" Gil spoke up as they finally paddled into the cattails along the south end of the lake. "I'm sure glad we didn't have to go any farther down the creek to find the railroad grade."

"Me too," Jug puffed. "And speaking of bears, I could eat one now."

"Just bring us one, and we'll cook it for you, won't we Ann?" Lori challenged him.

"I'll bring you one just as soon as I get time!" Jug promised.

Gil knew the girls didn't have much to worry about. It would be a long time before they would have to cook a bear for Jug.

At last they cleared the cattails, and moving into open water, a south west breeze helped push them toward the camp.

Three quarters of the way across the lake, Jug yelled, "Here comes the truck. Hope Uncle Jim got my gallon of chocolate cherry ice cream that I ordered."

"Don't hold your breath waiting for it," Ann warned him. "I don't have time to go to a funeral right now." Minutes later, they pulled up on the shore and after securing the canoe, they headed for the kitchen.

"Hey. Just in time," Uncle Jim called as they approached. "Let's unload our new frig and get it plugged in."

Jumping up in the back of the truck, Jim asked. "You guys want the bottom or the top?"

"Stay there," Gil responded. "We can get this end." Moments later the frig sat in it's place and Gil plugged it in.

"I'll get the packing material out of the inside," Jug told them. "So we can get the ice cream in here before it melts," he joked.

"Well Jug," Aunt Mary spoke up. "I felt sorry for you knowing that you're wasting away almost to nothing, so I did buy you some ice cream."

"Aunt Mary, you're the greatest!" he squealed and ran over and gave her a big hug. "At least I've got one in this crowd that feels sorry for me."

Later, as they sat down to eat, Jim asked, "How did you guys make out today?"

"Well, we did find the town this afternoon," Gil reported.

"It's strange," Ann told her father. "There's a cemetery way out there in the woods. People were buried there over a hundred years ago."

"But the strange thing is," Jug interrupted. "Most of the buildings are not falling down like everybody told us they would be," he explained. "There's a sign that's loose on the grocery store, and one old barn that's falling down, but otherwise what we saw looked to be in pretty good shape."

"Do you think someone has been using it for a deer hunting camp?" Uncle Jim asked.

"There are no signs of it," Gil answered. "But we really

didn't have much time to look around. The only thing we know for sure is that there was a little town there at one time, and it sure hasn't rotted into the ground."

"That is strange," Jim agreed. "Usually a roof only lasts about twenty five or thirty years. If the trains stopped fifty years ago and everyone moved away, they surely wouldn't have lasted this long."

"One of the houses was brick," Gil spoke up. "It must have been a pretty fancy house when it was built."

"The strangest thing I saw," Lori told them, "Was the one across from the brick house, had curtains on the windows! Who ever heard of curtains in a ghost town?"

"What house?" Jug interrupted. "I didn't see any house with curtains. Did you Gil?'

"That one on the side street across from the brick house!" Lori defended herself. "You saw them didn't you, Ann?"

"I hadn't thought about it before, but now that I think about it, it did have curtains."

"Oh, you guys are just making up that story to try to get me to think I'm goofy," Jug moaned. "But I know what I saw."

"You were thinking about all that chocolate cherry ice cream you were going to eat tonight and you just couldn't keep your mind on exploring," Ann shot back.

"You just wait and see when we go back there," Jug scoffed. "Then we'll see who's right."

Gil was silent. There had been something different about the house, but he couldn't explain what it was. But did it really have curtains? He hadn't noticed, but then, a girl would be more likely to notice things like that. He hadn't thought much about returning to the ghost town when they left it that afternoon, but the more they talked, the more he knew there would have to be a return trip soon. Meanwhile, there were more urgent things that would need their attention. Exploration would have to wait, for now.

"Let's get those light fixtures up in the bunkhouses," Gil suggested. "It's clouding up in the west, so we'd better get it done before it gets dark."

An hour later, thunder clouds had piled up over the lake and Uncle Jim called, "Let's make sure the canoes are tied down up high and dry. We don't want them to blow away."

"Ok," Jug answered. "It looks like we're going to have a good old storm tonight."

"Going to have some wind too," Jim predicted. "Just look at the way those thunder clouds are swirling around." Suddenly, across the lake a flash of lightning cut across the sky and a second later thunder shook the clearing in the trees.

"'Look at the top of the trees whip around over on the other side of the lake," Jug called, coming back from securing the canoes.

The muffled roar of wind and rain began to build as it crossed the lake, and the water was whipped into a mad frenzy. "Wouldn't want to be out there now," Gil yelled above the roar of the wind that was now moving into the great trees surrounding the camp. Moments later, wind driven raindrops the size of dimes began to pelt down on the camp with a vengeance.

Gil moved to a window away from the storm and Lori stepped up beside him. "Water's coming off the eaves like a river," he spoke into her ear so she could hear over the noise.

"The yard looks like a big lake," Lori added. "I wonder how much longer it will last?"

"At the rate it's coming down, it probably won't last too long," he assured her. "If it does, we'll float away in all this water."

A few minutes later, the wind began to let up and the rain slowed it's pace. Finally about nine o'clock the sky began to lighten and Jug called, "I can see a streak of bright red sun trying to peak through the clouds in the west." Soon, the setting sun turned the remaining clouds into a blaze of color.

A damp mist hung over the lake the next morning as the sun tried to rise over the forest. The rain had left everything drenched and dripping and the cooler air that followed had turned the vapors into whips of fog rising from the forest floor. Gil pulled on a heavy shirt as he stepped outside. " We'd better light up the fireplace this morning," he told Jug as they headed for the kitchen.

Soon smoke began to rise from the tall chimney in the dining room and the camp slowly came to life once more. "What's on for today?" Jug inquired as they set the table for breakfast.

"I want to see if we can get a temporary well driven so we can have running water, Uncle Jim replied. "We'll have to have someone come in and put in a bigger well later, but we need to get a water heater hooked up and some bathrooms fixed up with running water. The old outhouses have served their purpose so far, but if we're going to have a gang of kids here, we have to have something better."

"How do we go about driving a well?" Gil questioned. "How can you tell when you hit water?"

"I bought a well point at the hardware yesterday. It has a lot of holes in it that are covered by a very fine screen. It's pointed on one end so it can be driven into the ground, and the other end is threaded so we can add more pipe to it as we drive it down," Uncle Jim told them. "When we hit water, it runs through the screen into the pipe.

"We can tie a big fishing sinker to a string and drop it down the pipe. It'll go *plunk* when it hits the water, and if you mark your line at that point, you can tell how far down the water is.

"That doesn't sound too complicated," Jug responded. "How deep are we going to have to go?"

"That's the big question," Jim told the boys. "Sometimes in this part of the country, it's not too far down to bedrock. We need to get down past twenty feet so we don't just get surface water. If we hit rock at fifteen feet, then we'll have to get a well driller to come in and drill down through the rock into a pocket of water."

"I'll need a power saw," Jim called later when they were ready to start on the well. "We need to cut a hole in the floor big enough for us to get through when we need to. If we put the well inside, then it won't freeze when the weather gets cold."

"That sounds like a good idea," Gil agreed. He laid the saw down and plugged it into a wall plug.

"We'll just cut this square right out of the floor," Jim told them as the saw began to bite into the wood.

Gil turned to the pipe. The well point was not very long. "We'll have to add a five foot length of pipe so it will stick up above the floor, won't we?"

"That's right," Jim replied. "But be sure to put some of that pipe sealer on the threads before you screw it together. Then there's a drive coupling that goes on the top end of the pipe. It's a lot heavier than the others, so it can take the beating we're going to give it."

Done screwing the pipe together, Gil put the point end down into the hole in the floor and stood the pipe upright. "Ok, now what?" he asked.

"Grab that driver, Jug." He pointed to what looked like a thirty inch long piece of pipe with handles welded on it. One end of the driver was open but the other had a cap on it.

"Just slip the open end over the well pipe and we'll get one of us on each side. Then we'll lift the driver up and bang it down on the well pipe as hard as we can." Jim told the boys.

"Gil, if you can hold the pipe straight up and down, Jug and I will start driving. We'll hit it a few blows and then we'll trade places, so we don't get too tired."

With the first blow of the driver, the pipe settled into the dirt several inches. "We'll drive it down a couple of feet, then we can put a level on it to make sure it's going straight down."

When two feet of pipe was in the ground, Gil checked it with the level and changed places with Jug. "It won't take us long at this rate," Gil suggested.

"No, if it would keep going down like that, it wouldn't take long. But I've got a feeling it'll drive a lot harder the farther we go," Uncle Jim told the boys. "Ok, let's see if we can drive it down to the floor so we can add another piece."

Minutes later the pipe was driven down as far as they could drive it and Jim said, "Get the pipe wrenches. We have to take the drive coupling off and add another piece of pipe."

Jug quickly removed the coupling and Gil added a piece of pipe. Working together they tightened the joints and put the drive coupling back on the top. "We're ready," Jug called. Then the boys grabbed the driver and down went the pipe into the ground.

"Ok, that ought to do it," Jim called as the top of the pipe drew near to the floor.

Pausing to catch his breath, Gil asked? "Do you think we're into the water yet?"

"Well, we're only about twelve feet into the ground, but with the lake so close, we might be," he suggested. "Let's drop our sinker and line down the pipe and we'll see what we have."

Picking up the line in one hand, Gil dropped the weight down with the other. The sinker pulled the line down as it fell, then went *ker-plunk* and stopped moving. "Sounds like there's water down there."

"Pull up the extra line, then bob the line up and down until it plunks in the water every time you drop it," Uncle Jim instructed. "That way you can tell exactly how far down the water is."

Gil followed his directions, then holding the line tight with his fingers, he pulled on the line and walked backwards until the sinker came out of the pipe and dropped on the floor. "Grab a tape measure and check how far it is."

"Eight and one half feet," Jug reported.

"That's good," Uncle Jim replied. "If the water doesn't come up high enough in the pipe, the pump won't work. Now if we can just get it down another fifteen or twenty feet without hitting bedrock, we'll have it made."

Perspiration began to trickle down their faces as blow after blow rang the pipe, slowly driving it into the ground. "This is beginning to be just like work!" Jug puffed as they added another section of pipe.

When they traded places again, Gil commented, "It's really driving hard now. It hardly moves when you hit it. Will it get to going so hard we can't drive it?" But finally it was time to add another piece.

"We may be in a streak of clay," Jim explained as they added another piece of pipe. "If we can get this piece and one more driven down, we'll see if we can pump it. If we're still in the water then, that should be deep enough."

The pipe was driving hard. "Let's hit it twenty times and then switch places," Jim suggested. Finally it was down and they rested a moment before driving the last piece. As they began to drive again, the pipe began to drive easier and with each blow it would drop a half inch. "We must be back in the sand again."

Done driving, Gil asked, "Want to check the water level?"

"Yes," Jim answered. "I borrowed a pitcher pump from the hardware so we can hand pump it. If the hand pump won't work on it, then an electric pump won't work either," he explained.

Gil quickly dropped the line down the pipe again and called, "Between eight and nine feet. Is that too far to pump it?"

"It should be good," Uncle Jim answered. "Unless the point is in clay, but I think it's probably in sand, the way that piece drove. Ok, let's get the pump and we can screw it right on the top of the well pipe."

After the pump was tightened, Jug grabbed the handle and started to pump rapidly. "Hey, I'm not getting any water," he moaned. "What do we do now?"

"Get Aunt Mary's pail of spring water. Then while one of you pumps, the other can pour water into the top of the pump," Jim instructed.

Gil poured water in while Jug worked the handle, and after just a few strokes, water began gushing out of the spout.

"Hey, we did it," Jug screamed.

"It looks kind of dirty," Gil spoke up.

"It'll take a little pumping to get the clay and fine sand worked out of the screen, but it should clear up soon," Jim told them.

"After we've pumped it for a few minutes, we'll take a sample of it in to town. They'll test it to make sure it's all right. Then we're ready for a pump, and running water."

After a few minutes of pumping, the water had cleared up a lot and Uncle Jim caught some in a pail. "Well boys, it sure looks good to me, and it smells a lot better than city water. Let's catch some in that bottle there, and after dinner we'll take it in and have it checked."

Just then Aunt Mary called, "Lunch will be ready as soon as you guys get cleaned up."

As they sat eating, Jim suggested, "When we go in to town this afternoon, you guys could check with the county clerk's office. She might have some aerial pictures of the area. They usually take the pictures when the leaves have fallen off the trees, so things show up quite well."

"Do you think they could tell us if anyone lives there?" Jug asked.

"They will have a record of who owns it and who pays the taxes on it. If you take the old map along, they should be able to find it with little problem," he told them

CHAPTER VII
HAVE YOU SEEN JOE?

Pulling up in front of the county offices, Jim headed for the door that said, County Health Department. As the four teens were climbing out of the back of the truck, Gil noticed the sheriff coming out of the post office with a handful of mail and called, "Hello Sheriff. How are you today?"

"Great," he replied. "And how are you young ladies?" He spoke to the girls. "Are these fellows getting you involved in the middle of another mystery today?"

"Well, I guess we're all in it together," Lori laughed. "We were all there when Gil found that jar of coins, so we really didn't have a lot of choice whether to be in it or not."

"And we found a spooky old town in the woods on the other side of the lake yesterday afternoon," Ann informed him.

The sheriff's eyebrows raised in surprise. "What do you mean, you found an old town?"

Gil reached into his pocket and pulled out the old map. "It was a town they called "Danesville," he told the sheriff.

The sheriff studied the map for a moment, then shaking his head he spoke in disbelief, "I've been sheriff for ten years, and I never knew there was a town in that part of the county."

"Uncle Jim said the county clerk might be able to give us

some information on who owns the land there in that town," Gil explained.

"I'm sure she can," He replied. "Let me give this mail to my secretary, and then I'll introduce you to her." Entering the county building, the sheriff dropped off his mail, then pointed down the hall. "Clerk's office is this way. Just follow me."

Entering an open door on the right, a middle aged lady greeted him.

"Afternoon, Mrs. Roalfe. I've got some detectives here that need some help, if you have the time."

She turned and greeted them with a smile. "Time, Sheriff? Things are so slow here today, that I can't find a thing to do other than clean up, and I already cleaned up day before yesterday! You know, I can only clean up so much. I can't even get any dust on my dust rag," she smiled.

"I know it," the sheriff replied. "Life sure can be difficult at times," he laughed.

"Now young ladies, and you fellows too. What can I do for you?

Gil spread the old map out on the counter and said, "We would like to find out some information about who owns this land, here where this old town used to be."

"That shouldn't be too hard," she responded. "I'm sure glad you came along to rescue me from my boredom. This place has been dead all week, but I have to stay around whether there's something to do or not," she sputtered. "Ok, let's go check the books. You can all come with me."

She walked to a table, where a large book lay open on top of it. "Aerial maps of the whole county are in this book," she explained. She looked at Gil's map first, then checked the index in the front of the big book on the table. Flipping the pages open, she found the one she wanted. Then spreading it out on the table, she asked, "This look anything like it?"

Gil stepped closer and began to study the blueprint colored pages. In the center, was a dark spot shaped like a potato. "This is our lake, isn't it?" he observed. "Look, there's the shadows of the bunkhouses and the dining hall!"

"And here's the creek coming out of the lake that we canoed down yesterday," Lori observed. "Look, it turns back to the east and then runs into the river a little farther down."

Silently they studied the map. Gil turned his attention to the area where the railroad went from the creek to the old town. "I think this is where the railroad crossed the creek and headed west," he pointed to the map. " There's a faint line here leading from the creek to this swampy area to the west where the road is clearly visible."

"Hey, I think you're right," Jug agreed. "Now where are those buildings at the old town?"

Lori's finger settled on the page where there were a group of dark spots in the picture. "What are these?" she asked Mrs. Roalfe.

Looking to where Lori was pointing, she smiled and said, "Oh, those dark spots are evergreen trees and the shadows that they make. They take the pictures when the hardwoods don't have any leaves on them. That way they get the location of all the natural landmarks which helps when the land is sold or being divided into smaller pieces."

Gil studied the spot Lori had pointed out. The faint line of the old railroad crossed through the place where the evergreens grew. Looking closer, he made a discovery. "Does it look to you guys like some of these dark spots are round and some are square?"

"What are you getting at?" Ann questioned her cousin.

"See this spot, and this one, and here's another? They seem to be more square. Then here's a line of spots that aren't nice and round, either. And see, this line is at a ninety degree angle with the others. Do you suppose these could be the buildings in the town? See this one? It's round on this side, but the other side is quite square, like a house with a big evergreen tree growing on one end."

"I think you might be right," Jug agreed. "And they seem to be in about where the town should be."

"Find what you're looking for?" Mrs. Roalfe asked. "We think so," Gil told her. "Is there any way you could tell us who owns this property?"

"Oh, that's no problem," she assured them. "I just need to get some numbers off the page. Picking up a notepad she copied some numbers from the page, then reached under the counter and pulled out a record book. Opening it, she flipped through the pages until she found the numbers she was looking for.

"Hiawatha Forest Products owns that land. In fact, they own all the land between the lake and the river, and a lot more besides that around here."

"Well, I guess that's another dead end," Jug sputtered. "But how can they own all of it when there used to be a town there? What happened to the town?" Mrs. Roalfe explained, "When people don't pay the taxes on their land, then the county has to put it up for sale to pay the taxes. Often people who own property around that land can pick it up for a very reasonable price."

"Was there someone special you were looking for, or are you just interested in a real ghost town?" She asked.

"We're looking for a man by the name of Joe Green," Gil spoke up. "A couple of old fellows said he lived in Danesville years ago, and we wanted to try to find out what happened to him, if we could," he explained.

"Well, as long as I don't have much else to do anyway, let me see what I can find out."

She turned and stepped into another room at the back of the office. A moment later returned with several record books and laid them up on the counter.

"This is the property tax roll from ten years ago," she told them, and opening the book, she skimmed through the names. "Nothing here."

"We'll have to go farther back." Laying that book aside she searched two more notebooks with the same results. Picking up the forth book she explained "This one is from forty years back. Let's see what we can find."

Searching through the names, suddenly she called out, "Ok, here we are! A Dr. John Morgan owned 80 acres right in that area."

She turned the page, and her finger stopped on the very first entry. Even reading the book bottom side up, Gil could read the name. "Joe Green," she spoke the name. "Yes, he did own land, just where the old timers told you. But that was forty years ago," she added.

"Does it give any more information about him?" Lori inquired.

"He owned three hundred and twenty acres there on the edge of town. And let's see, it gives his address as a post office box in Hemlock corners. That's about twenty miles from here."

"That's great," Gil told her. "At least, now we know that he did own quite a chunk of ground there. But, what do you think happened to him? I wonder if he moved away, or what?"

"I have no way of knowing that," Mrs. Roalfe replied. "The only other thing I could do is check the deed to the property. There's a slight chance it might give some more details."

Again, she disappeared into the back room. A couple of minutes later, she returned with a file folder. Opening it, she began to check the contents carefully. Finally, she pulled out a paper and began to read, *This indenture made between, Joseph Green and Elizabeth Green, his wife, party of the first part, and Hiawatha Forest Products, party of the second part - -.*

"What's that mean?" Jug interrupted.

"It simply means that the Greens sold their land to Hiawatha Forest Products."

"They sold 320 acres of land for $27,000. But wait," she pointed to the paper, "It says the Green's would keep a lease on the house and ten acres of land as long as they lived."

"They could use it like they owned it, but Hiawatha would have to pay the taxes on it. When the Greens passed away, Hiawatha would own it," she explained. "The Greens just had a place to live for the rest of their lives."

"Then, he *could* have lived there after he sold the land," Gil concluded.

"That's right," Mrs. Roalfe agreed. "You could check with the post office over to Hemlock Comers. Maybe, they could tell you when that box was last used by Mr. Green."

"Well, we sure thank you for all the help you've given us," Gil told her.

"Oh, it wasn't much," she protested.

"We definitely have a lot more information than we had before," Lori assured her. "We really do appreciate it."

Leaving the office, Lori spoke softly, "I wrote down Joe Green's post office box number."

"Good thinking," Gil complimented her.

As they walked by the open door of the sheriff's office, a voice called from inside, "Hey you guys, did you learn anything?"

Gil stopped and filled the sheriff in on what they had learned. "All we really have is a post office box number," Gil concluded.

"Let me make a note of that," the sheriff told him.

"The next time I'm over that way, I'll check it out."

Catching up with Uncle Jim, he told them, "The water checked out ok, so let's head over to the hardware and pick up the water pump. They're supposed to have it all ready for us."

Later, heading for home Lori asked, "Is there any possibility that Joe Green could be living in Hemlock Comers where his post office box was?"

"I don't know what to think," he told her. "My dad was a baby when Joe sold the land to Hiawatha, and Joe wasn't a boy then. Those two old men we talked to there in front of the hardware looked like they might be eighty years old. And they said that Joe was older than they were."

"I see what you mean," Lori responded. "What are we going to do now? Is there really any need to go back to the ghost town?"

"Probably not. Still, that's the last place that we know where he lived." Gil reasoned. "The way I see it, we only have two possibilities of finding him. Either we find him still living in the ghost town, or over at Hemlock Comers. If we don't turn up anything there, then I'm ready to forget about it."

"I guess the sheriff is the only one who can get that information from the post office, isn't he?" she asked. "And if that's the case, the only option we have left is to go back to the ghost town."

"Yes, I guess you're right," Gil agreed. "Let's check out the old town the first chance we get."

Back at the camp once more, they went to work installing the pump. "It makes it a lot easier if the water is close to the surface, like it is here," Uncle Jim explained. 'We just have to :fasten the pump to the pipe, pour a little water in the pump, and plug it in."

Gil knew there would need to be a lot more plumbing done in the near future, but for today, they just needed to get the pump running and the new water heater operating. Camping in the wilderness was fun for a change, but heating water over a wood fire and washing clothes by hand was hard work any way you looked at it.

"You know, Jug, it's fun and refreshing to swim in the lake, but a good hot shower would feel good too," Gil suggested.

"You can say that again," Jug agreed.

By seven-thirty, the pump and the heater were installed and ready to turn on the power. "Jim looked around one last time, then called, "Turn on the pump and let's see if we can get some water."

Just as Gil threw the pump switch, Aunt Mary called, "Somebody's coming down the trail."

"It's the sheriff," Ann reported. "He's got his boat behind the car."

Meanwhile, the pump hummed for a moment and then slowed slightly as it started to pump up water pressure in the tank. "Pressure gauge says it's up to ten pounds," Jug reported, and a few seconds later the motor clicked off.

"Let's turn on that outside faucet that we installed. We'll let it run for a few minutes to clear the water up, before we fill the water heater," Uncle Jim instructed the boys. "Why don't you boys see what the sheriff wants."

"Going fishing?" Jug called to the sheriff.

"Not tonight," he explained. "I wanted to get this boat out here tonight. I have to pick up my friend at the airport first thing in the morning. Maybe tomorrow night we'll get a chance to get out for a while."

"You've got a nice boat," Gil told the sheriff.

Yes, he replied. "The county didn't have any money to buy a boat, and mine was getting pretty well worn out, so I decided to buy this one, and the County pays me when I use it for them"

"Is there a place where I can back the trailer in the lake without getting stuck in the mud?" he asked.

"Swing your car around and back up right over there," Gil

Frank Austin

pointed to an open spot between two trees. "The lake bottom drops off quite quickly there. I think it'll work for you."

Gil directed him as he backed into the lake. "That's good," he called when the trailer began to disappear in the water."' think it'll slide off now."

The sheriff quickly loosened the ropes holding the boat and let it slip out into the water. "If you'll hang on to this rope, I'll pull the trailer out from under it." Getting into his car, he pulled the trailer ahead well up on to the grass and shut it off.

"Boy, I like your boat," Jug told the sheriff. "I can see where that would make fishing a lot easier than paddling a canoe around the lake. Inboard motor. Nice."

"Well, it isn't your average row boat," the sheriff laughed. "Lots of power, and designed to run in very shallow water. No propeller to catch in the weeds, just a jet of water to drive it. When I'm chasing a crook, I can't afford to get hung up in shallow water. Jump in, and I'll take you for a little spin."

"Hey, that's great," Jug answered and started climbing in.

Moments later, they were circling the lake. It seemed like it took only seconds to get to the creek on the south end of the lake. As they glided across the water, the sheriff explained how to maneuver the craft around. "I want you boys to know how to run the boat properly. You won't get hurt if you use a little common sense. If you guys want to go fishing, I want you to use my boat. I'll let you know when I'm going to need it," he told them.

"Are you sure?" Gil questioned. "You must have a lot of money in it."

"Oh, I've got some money in it, but I do want you to use

it," he told them. "You fellows have proven to me that you are trustworthy. So if I show you how it operates, then you won't hurt it. After all, I didn't buy it just to let it set around. Besides, in this part of the country, the lakes are frozen over nearly half of the year. If we're going to use it, now's the time to do it."

It was almost time for bed when Uncle Jim opened his Bible and began reading, *But seek ye first the kingdom of God, and his righteousness; and all these things shall be added unto you.* "All around him, Jesus and his disciples could see people struggling to get the things they wanted, food, clothing, and shelter from the cold. Others struggled for wealth, for power, and importance."

Jim continued, "The same struggle is all around us today. People lie, and steal from others. Sometimes they will even kill for what they want. You see, the world never guarantees anything. Even now, there are places in the world where people are starving to death."

"In other places, wars are taking lives, destroying homes and robbing people of their jobs, and a way to provide for their families. But it doesn't have to be that way. There is a very simple way for us to be sure that all these things that we need will be taken care of. That simple way is just give control of our lives to God and let him lead us each step of the way."

"God designed each of us even before he created the world. Way back then, he knew what our needs would be. And today, seeing that he owns and controls the universe that he designed, he is certainly able to provide every need we have whether it is great or small."

When their devotions were over, Jug asked, "What's up for tomorrow?"

"I have to run over to Sault Ste. Marie to meet with some people," Jim replied. Then I have to pick up some supplies that I can't get in these small towns around here. I'm going to have to leave early, and I hope I can get back before dark."

"Mary is going to stay here at camp, so this will give you guys some time for yourselves. If you decide to do any more exploring, you'll have to check it out with her," he told them.

"I can read your mind just by looking at your face," Lori turned and spoke softly to Gil.

"What are you talking about," he questioned.

"You're thinking about going back to that ghost town, aren't you?"

A smile crossed his face, "I can' t say the thought didn't cross my mind." He paused a moment, then asked, "What do you think about it?"

"It's a long walk, but I guess that's the only way we'll ever know whether everyone has really left that place."

Gil nodded his head. "Maybe if we fixed a picnic lunch and left by nine o'clock, we would have plenty of time to check out the whole town without having to hurry."

"Hey, are we being left out of some plans?" Jug interrupted.

"Just talking about making a trip back to Danesville in the morning," Gil explained. "What do you think?"

"Been thinking about it ever since we left town this afternoon. I still don't think there were any curtains on those windows," he shook his head.

"There certainly was," Ann elbowed him in the ribs.

"You just need glasses so you can see them!"

"We can take a picnic lunch," Gil told them. "If we wear our backpacks we ought to be able to get everything in them that we need."

"Sounds great," the others agreed.

CHAPTER VIII
THE SEARCH

xcitement ran high at breakfast the next morning as they began to prepare for their trip back to the ghost town.

The girls were busy preparing the picnic lunch that they were taking with them. "Can't let Jug help with this job," Ann spoke up. "He'd have it all eaten before he left." She often joked about Jug, but in reality they were very good friends.

Meanwhile, Gil and Jug were gathering the other things they would need to take. Gil went through his list, "Compass, matches, first aid kit, screwdriver, small tools," he checked them off.

"I've got a flashlight," Jug added. "Survey ribbon, bug repellant. All we lack is the food."

"I guess if we get that packed in, then we'll be set to go," Gil finished his checklist and laid it on the table.

Ten minutes later, they were loaded in the canoe and headed across the lake towards the creek. "It's going to be another beautiful day," Gil observed as they headed the canoe towards the cattails along the south side of the lake. It had been cool in the shade of the big maples at the camp, but once they cleared the shade along the shore, the sun warmed the air quickly.

Geese, ducks, and other waterfowl were busy around the lake. It was summertime, and they had lots of things to do. "Oh, look at that duck over there," Lori nodded toward shore. "Her babies look like six little fuzz balls swimming along behind their mother."

The canoe quickly cut across the surface of the lake leaving behind them an ever widening V in the water. Minutes later, Gill called, "Creek's a little to the left!" and they slipped silently into it.

Moving on down the stream, they kept a steady pace stopping only long enough to trim off some low overhanging branches. "When we get to where that tree is tipped over in the creek," Gil suggested. "Let's see if we can cut the top off. I think the current will carry it out of the way."

"Good idea," Jug replied, and soon guided the canoe to the bank of the stream by the fallen tree.

Gil grabbed up a saw and climbed out on the bank. "I think I can walk out on the trunk far enough to cut the top off," he explained. A little over half way across, he paused and grabbed a sturdy branch with his left hand. Taking the saw in his right hand, he began to saw away at the tree top. A couple of minutes later, the top settled into the water, hesitated there a moment, and then was carried away in the current.

"Just stay where you are. We'll bring the canoe around," Jug told him, stepping back in to the canoe.

Five minutes later they stood on top of the hill, ready to head down the trail. "Look," Ann pointed. "The ribbons are still there."

"It looks almost like orange lights hanging on the branches," Lori observed.

"Ok, everyone ready?" Gil asked.

"All set," they replied, then headed into the woods.

Gil and Lori led the way. None of them were couch potatoes. Gil knew they wouldn't have to stop and rest too many times before they got to the town. "At least now we don't have to stop and hunt for the trail," he spoke to Lori. Ahead, there was always a bright ribbon or two to guide them on their way.

Suddenly, Lori reached and touched his arm. "Look," she pointed down the trail. A doe was standing partially hidden by a tree. She looked almost like a foam hunting target that hunters use for practice shooting.

The doe stood motionless looking at them. Now and then her ears would move slightly as she listened, and her tail twitched as she tried to scare away a hungry fly.

Then, she turned her head and looked back, almost like she was being followed. A second later, a little spotted fawn stepped out of the bushes into the trail.

"Look. There's another one!" Lori whispered as a second fawn bounded out beside the first one, then stopped.

They looked frozen in time as they stood there, looking toward the four teens. Then suddenly, like the fawns could stand there no longer, they took off with a bound, circling and leaping as they frolicked across the forest floor. The mother watched for a second, then moved on and followed the fawns into some brush.

Pushing on, a blue jay began to scream off in the direction the deer had gone, Like a tattletale at school yelling, Someone is coming! Someone is coming! Gil thought. A couple hundred yards farther a grouse crossed the trail ahead, followed by a dozen peeping chicks hurrying to keep up.

"It looks quite bare and lifeless here under these big trees," Gil told Lori. "I can understand how deer and the birds can find enough to eat now, but just imagine it being twenty degrees below zero and three feet of snow on the ground. How can they find enough to eat then?"

"When you put it that way, it does seem impossible," Lori agreed. "But remember, Jesus told his disciples that he even watches over the sparrows."

"Yes, that's true," Gil responded thinking about the verse Uncle Jim had read last night. "I guess I'd never looked at it that way before. If God designed everything before he created it, then the forest was designed to feed the creatures that live in it, even when it gets twenty degrees below zero."

"I guess then, if God is wise enough and strong enough to take care of his creation, then we ought to let him take care of our needs!" Lori reasoned. "You can sure see things with a new perspective when you get out here in God's creation," she concluded.

As they paused to rest for a moment at the cemetery Jug asked, "What's the plan when we get there?"

"I was thinking, maybe we should split up and find out just how many buildings there are in town, and if anything special stands out," Gil told him. "If you and Ann want to take one side of the trail, Lori and I will take the other side. We should be able to do that before noon. Let's meet back where the two streets cross there by the old train station."

"That sounds like a good idea," Jug told his friend. Turning to Ann, he said, "We'll take the right side of the tracks, if you don't mind."

They moved on down the trail to the cross street, then separated to begin their search. "We'll see you back here in a little while," Jug called and they turned and headed down the street.

"Let's go on to the west until we get to the end of the houses," Gil suggested. Then we'll work our way back here."

They took their time as they went, making mental notes as they walked along. "Does it seem a little strange to you that the houses look like they've been kept up?" Gil asked. "Look at the shingles on that house. Some of them look like they have been replaced not many years ago."

"Yes, it does," Lori agreed. "But then, look at the bushes and trees in the yards. It looks like no one has cared for them in a long time."

Pushing on, they passed a dozen houses and two more cross streets before they ran into the forest again. "Well, I guess that's about it," Gil reasoned. "Let's check what's down the cross streets and work our way back to the depot."

Crisscrossing from one building to another, they headed back to the east. "Doesn't look like there's much here," Gil commented. "Just a few houses with their windows all boarded up."

"Like they were going on a long vacation but expected to return one day," Lori observed.

"If we're going to find anything, we're going to have to find it soon, because there's not much town left to explore." Gil suggested.

"It doesn't look like anything but deer have used these streets for years," Lori said. "It's like it has been picked out of another century."

Coming to the last street Gil spoke, "What do you think? Do you see anything we need to take a longer look at?"

"Nothing looks very promising," she answered. "It's for sure, nobody's living in these houses."

Pausing at the comer, they looked down the street toward the brick house they had seen before. "It looks like it would be a beautiful house if the trees and shrubs were trimmed up around it," Lori said softly.

"Yes," Gil agreed, then out of the comer of his eye he saw something moving off to their left. Turning, he said, "Jug and Ann are headed back. Let's go see what they found out. We can check out that brick house after we eat."

"I hadn't thought about it, but I am hungry. Maybe I'm getting Jug's disease," she laughed.

Joining the others, Gil called out, "What did you find?"

"A dozen houses with the windows boarded up," Jug reported. "Doesn't look like anybody's been around for a long time. "What'd you guys find?"

"About the same," Gil answered. "Didn't have time to look at that brick house at the end of this street. That's about the only thing that appears interesting enough to take another look at now. It shouldn't take too long to check it out."

"You guys ready to eat?" Lori questioned.

"Am I ready to eat?" Jug spoke up quickly. "I thought you'd never ask."

"Let's go sit there on the depot steps," Ann suggested and they headed that way.

Stepping up to the dock Gil reached out and tried the big

door. To his surprise it swung in with hardly a squeek. "Wow, that startled me," he said. "I thought for sure it would be locked."

Inside, several empty shipping boxes sat around the large open room. A pot bellied stove sat on one end, with its smoke pipe disappearing into a chimney high overhead. What appeared to be a small office, had been partitioned off at the other end. Outside the small room hung a chalk board displaying the letters, TRAIN SCHEDULE, across the top. On it was written, "Last train, Wed. June 10."

"It's hard to believe those words were written there a half century ago," Gil said.

"Hey, you guys," Jug protested. "I'm slowly starving while you guys are lost in time fifty years ago! If we don't eat pretty soon, you're going to have to add another marker to that cemetery down the road."

He grabbed an empty shipping box, slid it out on the dock and tipped it on one side. "There's your table! Now do you want me to pray for this food, or are you going to?" He cried in mock anger, spreading the food from his backpack out on the crate.

"Well as long as you're going to get mad about it, we'll break away from our busy schedule and join you," Gil told his friend. "And seeing that you are at the point of death, I will personally ask the blessing on the food."

A couple of minutes later, Jug picked up a sandwich and took a big bite. "Oh, this is my favorite kind of sandwich," he said.

"I thought you told Aunt Mary that her burgers were your favorite food the other night," Gil challenged.

"Them too!" he added. Stuffing the other half sandwich in his mouth, he then reached for another.

As he ate, Gil noticed some writing on the side of the crate. The wood had turned dark over the years and the letters were somewhat faded but he could still make them out. *Smith's General Store, Danesville, Mich.* "When we get done here, let's take a look at the store," he suggested.

Heading toward the faded sign on the front of the store, Jug called, "I'm going to buy me a bag of candy!""I'll buy it for you if you'll eat itGill grinned. "I know how you love candy, but have you ever tried fifty year old candy?"

"Maybe the store's locked," Ann suggested.

Gil jumped up on the step and pulled the latch down with his thumb. "It's funny, nothing is locked," he spoke as the door swung in. Inside, the board covered windows didn't let much light in, but as his eyes grew accustomed to the darkness, he could make out shelves covering the outside walls from floor to ceiling.

"There's another door back here," Jug announced stepping to the opposite end of the store. "I'm going to see if we can get some more light in here." Once the door was open, a ray of sun coming through an open place high in the tree top penetrated into the building.

"That's better," Lori told them. "Now I can see to do my shopping."

Moving to the right, Gil could see that the store had been divided into two sections. One end had been used for hardware and the other for groceries. Walking to the hardware section, he discovered nail bins that still held a small amount of nails, and hooks and shelves that contained odds and ends of hardware.

Meanwhile Lori and Ann were in the grocery section. "Look here," Lori pointed to some big glass jars with six inch metal covers on them. "They must have held cookies. This one says ginger snaps, and over here sugar cookies."

Moving on, they came to similar, but smaller jars that had contained candy. "Jug's out of luck," Ann smiled. "The candy's all gone."

Various signs hung on the wall that were unfamiliar to Gil, but on the counter sat a *Cracker Jack* display, and high up on the wall was a *Baby Ruth* sign. "There are a few things that have been around for a long time," he commented.

Nearby stood two ancient meat coolers that once had held ice to keep their meat fresh. 'White tags with removable red numbers had once told the customers how much their steak was going to cost. "It's hard to imagine that people once lived here and bought their food right here in this little store," Jug observed.

"It's hard to imagine how this store could hold enough to supply the whole community," Lori added.

"They must have lived a much simpler life than we do." "We think we need to have running water and electricity in our homes, but these people never had those things. Life may have been simpler in some ways, but it must have been a lot harder too," Gil responded.

"I keep thinking, how could they stand it without the things that we have? They must have been very unhappy," Lori reasoned. "But then, the thought came to me, I know some people who have the latest of everything, and they're still not happy either."

Frank Austin

"Yes," Gil nodded. 'That's true.

"You guys about ready to go explore something else, seeing that they won't sell us any food here?" Jug called from across the room.

"I guess there's nothing more here that we need to see," Gil answered. "Shall we go check out that brick house?"

Stepping outside, they put on their backpacks. Just before heading toward the old brick house, Gil paused and pulled the old map from his pocket. "It looks like the whole town was centered around the railroad," he said pointing to the map. "See here, there are only a couple of unimproved roads running out just a mile or so from town. Looks like the railroad was everything to them."

"I wonder why nobody ever built a road into this town?" Ann questioned.

Gil studied the map for a moment. "Well, there's a lake to the north, the river and a large swamp on the east, and then the river curves around to the south. That leaves the west with some rivers and creeks flowing through it. The railroad was their link to the outside, and when it closed, there was no way for the people to make a living, so there wasn't much reason to stay."

CHAPTER IX
YOU RANG SIR?

eading south down the cross street, they came to a building on the right that was different from the others. "I wonder, could that have been a school house?" Ann questioned.

"It looks like it has a belfry on the roof," Gil observed. "Or maybe, it was a church, or both?"

"That' s a possibility," Lori agreed as they walked on. As they approached the brick house, they discovered the houses here were larger than the others in the town. "Must be the rich people lived on this street," Jug concluded.

The big brick house stood further back from the street than the others, and a concrete sidewalk ran from the street to the front porch. "'This one doesn't have boards nailed over the windows," Gil observed.

"It doesn't look so forsaken either," Ann added.

"What do you mean?" Jug asked.

"Well, the bushes and trees don't seem so overgrown, like they were taking over the place," Ann explained.

"I thought you were going to say it had curtains on the windows," Jug laughed.

"No! Not this one, dummy," Ann snapped. "It's the one across the street that has curtains on it."

Turning to look across the street, Jug's eyes almost popped out of his head. "It does have curtains! I thought you were pulling my leg. Whoever heard of a ghost town house with curtains?"

"Some ghosts are just more particular than others," Lori gave him a big "got ya" smile.

Gil turned toward the house with curtains. "It hasn't been too many years since that house was painted," he suggested. "And the trees and bushes have been trimmed and cared for. Hey look, there's a rocking chair on the front porch." He walked over to the porch, stepped up beside the chair and knocked loudly on the front door.

"You don't think someone is in there, do you?" Jug asked.

"You never know unless you knock," Gil replied. He knocked on the door again, and hearing no answer, he reached out and tried the knob. "Door's locked. That's funny," he stepped back to the ground. "Nothing else in town has been locked."

"What do you think that means?' Ann inquired.

"Probably nothing," he said.

Jug circled around to the back of house. "Hey," he called. "There's an axe leaning against the back porch. The blade looks like it has been used recently!"

Gil hurried around to join him. Then seeing nothing else unusual, he said, "Let's check out the brick house across the street."

They quickly moved across the street and followed the sidewalk to the front porch. Double doors with stained glass sidelights and a big brass door knocker stood before them as they stepped up on the porch.

Gil reached out and banged the knocker on the door. "I don't think anyone has knocked that thing in a long time," he suggested. "Feel the knob. It'd be smooth if it had been used much lately."

"Look at this. There's a nameplate here beside the door," Lori nodded. "Dr. John Morgan. Wasn't that the other land owner the county clerk mentioned to us the other day?"

"Yes, I think it was," Gil agreed, then reached up and banged the knocker again. "When I get a house, I'm going to have a knocker like that," he laughed.

Suddenly, the door swung open and a deep voice called, "You rang, sir?"

Startled, Gil jumped back, then quickly called out, "You turkey! How'd you get in there?"

Jug's laughter rang out through the doorway. "Got 'ya that time," he squealed. "The back door was unlocked. I'm sorry, but I couldn't resist."

The front entry was a large room with high ceilings, and along either side, chairs lined the walls. Fancy stained woodwork framed the two doors on the opposite wall Gil could see that the men who built this house had been skilled craftsmen. He stepped to the door on the right and turned the knob. Inside the room were several chairs and a small desk. Just beyond it, an open door revealed the doctor's examination room.

Entering the room, Lori called back, "It's funny, but his medical tools are still here, like he just disappeared." Gil stepped to the door and looked in. The doctor's medical bag sat unlatched on a chair. "It still has pills in it," he reported.

A door on the left caught Gil's attention. Walking to it, he swung it open. On the opposite wall wooden shutters had been closed over two tall windows, but a couple of missing slats let enough light in to tell that this had been the doctor's study. On the left, book filled shelves lined the walls from floor to ceiling. A great stone fireplace dominated the opposite wall and two overstuffed chairs were centered in front of it. Beside one chair stood a low table. A gas lamp stood on it beside an open book.

Moving closer, Gil picked up the book and looked at it. "The Doctor must have been a Christian! See, this is a Bible, and a lot of verses are underlined."

Lori stepped close and looked. "Yes, he must have been a Christian," she agreed.

They spent almost an hour wandering through the various rooms in the big house. "He must have used the place for a hospital as well as a home," Gil concluded when he discovered three smaller rooms, each containing a narrow bed in it. Finally, deciding they had seen enough, they headed for the front door and stepped outside.

"Well what do you think?" Jug asked. "We still don't know any more about Joe Green than when we came."

"I know it," Gil replied, disappointment showing in his voice. "If we could just find some indication that he was here or that he had died. Just anything would help."

"Records!" Lori interrupted. "Medical records!"

"What are you talking about?" Jug demanded.

"The doctor must have kept medical records. They might tell us something, if we could find them."

"Why didn't I think of that," Gil moaned. "Let's go back

and see what we can find." Moving inside once again, they soon discovered two large drawers in a cabinet that were full of records.

"This drawer starts with the M's," Lori reported.

Gil flipped through the other drawer and finally came to the G's. "Gable, Gage, Gentz, Gibbs." He read the names. "Gorby, Gould, Graff. Oh, here's Green." He opened the folder only to discover that the patient was Elizabeth Green. He pulled out the next folder and opened it.

"Hey, this is more like it!" he cried out.

The record covered a long period of time, but Gil soon discovered there weren't many entries. He read, "Patient cut himself, six stitches. Log rolled on toe, cut hole in toenail to relieve pressure. Removed wood splinters, three stitches."

The final entry, made only five years earlier seemed to sum up Joe's medical condition; "Complained of chest pains. Finally admitted his ladder slipped out from under him. Fell and bruised his ribs. Heart and blood pressure, fine." Then one final note, "The old goat's tough enough to live to be a hundred."

"Wow," Lori cried. "Then he must have lived here in this town! He must have been here when this entry was made."

"Yes," the others agreed.

"But he had to have some outside contact. A person just couldn't live totally isolated in this part of the country," Gil reasoned as he checked his watch. "Three o'clock. Well, I suppose we should start back before long. Let's put these things back where we found them, and then take a one last look around town."

Standing in the street again, Gil pulled the map from his pocket and opened it to the area where they were standing. "If the doctor and Joe both lived here until five years ago, then there had to be a way to get out for supplies," he reasoned, studying the map.

Suddenly his brows raised and he asked, "The river? Could the river have been their road outside?"

His eyes traced the course of the river as it zigzagged to the west. All at once it began to make some sense. The river passed through the little town of Hemlock Comers about ten miles from where they stood. Joe's post office box was in Hemlock Corners! he remembered.

"I'm going to check how far it is to the river," Gil announced and started walking toward the brush at the end of the street.

"I'm coming with you," Jug replied.

Not far beyond the two houses, the street ended and thick brush began. Gil was trying to decide just where the best path through the thicket was, when a narrow opening seemed to appear ahead. "Is this a trail?" he spoke stepping closer.

"Maybe it's a game trail," Jug suggested.

But as they came to it, they discovered that it was just wide enough for them to pass down single file. With Gil leading the way, and Jug following close behind, they moved down the trail about twenty five feet, then suddenly, Gil stopped.

"Look here," he pointed to a narrow stream beside them. "There must be a good sized spring there in those bushes. This stream runs into the river right over there," he pointed.

The narrow path led on to what looked like a boat dock, right on the edge of the stream. Jug squeezed up beside Gil. "It looks like the dock has been used very recently," he suggested. "Who do you suppose it could be?"

"That's what I'm wondering," Gil replied. "At least someone has been using this dock recently! Oh well, if there's nothing more here, let's go find the girls."

Joining the girls again, Gil told them, "Someone has been here very recently with a boat. The path in the bushes is well worn, so it wasn't just made by a passing fisherman."

"Do you th---," Lori started to speak, then suddenly held up her hands signaling them to be quiet. Softly she spoke, "I thought I heard something?"

They stood motionless, listening, but only the singing and chirping of the forest creatures could be heard. "I thought I heard a noise, like a motor," she whispered.

They paused for several seconds. Hearing nothing, Lori was about to say "I guess it was just my imagination," when the muffled, but unmistakable put putting of a small motor could be detected from the direction of the river.

"Quick, let's get out of sight," Gil ordered. "We don't want to scare them away if they're coming here." He headed for a large clump of brush near the brick house where they would be able to see, but not be seen.

"We should be able to stay out of sight here," he reasoned. "And if necessary we should be able to slip back into the woods and back to our boat without being seen."

The sound of the motor seemed to be getting nearer, then slowed down to a put-put. As it came closer, all at once the sound stopped.

After a couple of minutes, Ann whispered, "What happened to them?"

Gil opened his mouth to reply, then something moved near the path into the brush, and a second later a man stepped out of the bushes. He was tall and thin with a full head of snow white hair. It was evident that he was an old man, but he stood straight and walked with a spring in his step. Moving closer, they could hear him whistling a tune that was unfamiliar to them. He carried two grocery sacks in his sun bronzed arms and seemed to be heading toward the house with curtains on the windows.

"Do you think that could be Mr. Green," Lori whispered.

"I don't know," Gil whispered. "But it looks like he could fit the description"

"What are we going to do?" Jug asked. "If we go out there now, no telling what he would do."

"Right," Gil replied. "Let's wait until he gets in the house for a couple of minutes. Then maybe we can walk up and knock on the door."

"Sounds like a good idea," Jug responded.

The old man sat one grocery sack on the porch, then stepped up and unlocked the front door and disappeared inside. A couple of minutes later, he returned and carried the other sack inside, closing the door behind him.

"What's our plan," Jug spoke up.

"Well, the way I see it, if we all go up and knock on the door, he might feel intimidated by us. If I go alone, I might be more apt to get him to talk. He'll be able to see that I'm not carrying anything to hurt him with, and I'll be more at ease knowing you guys are in a safe place."

"But what if you get a bad reaction from him?" Jug asked.

"I don't think he'll react that way, but if I should need help, I'll give you a call. That should scare him off, if he thinks I've got help."

"Everyone ok with that?" he asked.

"Alright. I'm going to swing back around towards the depot. I'll come out on the street there, just in case he might be looking." Gil said.

The others nodded their approval, and he circled around behind the houses toward the depot. Pausing for a moment, he bowed his head and asked God to help him to do the right thing. Then he stepped out into the street.

Better not be in too much of a hurry, he told himself If I walk like I'm enjoying the scenery, he won't know I'm really looking for him. He walked slowly as if he'd just seen the area for the first time. He was within a half block of the house when all at once, the front door opened and the old man stepped out on the front porch. Holding a newspaper in his hand, he moved toward the rocking chair. He started to sit down, then noticed Gil standing in the street looking toward the school house.

The old man acted like he didn't know whether to hurry back inside or sit down. Gil turned and slowly began to walk down the street.

He took a few more steps before turning toward the old man, like he had just discovered that he was there on the porch. Raising his hand, he waved at the old fellow and called, "Hello there. How are you today?"

The old timer looked Gil over good before answering. Seeing no one else, he seemed to relax a little and answered,

"Oh, I'm alright." Then quickly, a scowl crossed his brow and he called, "Wha'cha doin' here in this woods all alone? Kid like ya could get lost in this forest!"

Gil knew he would have to reply carefully, or the interview would be over. "Well," he began. "I'm looking for a man who I was told, lived here a long time ago. A couple of elderly fellows in town said they used to know this man when they worked at the sawmill on the other side of the lake."

"How'd ya know 'bout the mill? Been closed for years. Road's all grown up now!"

"My uncle bought the old mill property this past winter. We're going to make it a camp for kids," Gil explained. "I really don't want to bother you, but I'd like to find out if this man is still alive. This place is the last lead we have left."

"What's 'is name?" he inquired, the look of suspicion slowly fading from his face.

"Name's Joe Green," Gil answered.

The old man sat down in the rocking chair, giving no sign that he'd ever heard the name before. He sat a full minute, then motioned for Gil to sit down on the edge of the porch. "Why ya looking for this man? Why'zit so important to find 'im?"

"Well, it's a long story, but I found something that I think belonged to him. If he's still alive, I'd like to return it to him."

"Now, why'd ya wan' ta do a thing like that?" The old man questioned. "Ya sure yer tellin' the truth?"

"Yes. I am," Gil replied patiently, resisting the urge to shout it at him. "It looked like it may have been important to this Joe Green, and all I want to do is return it to him," he assured the old man.

Suddenly, Gil sensed the old fellow knew more than he was letting on, and he asked, "Would you know if this Joe Green is still alive and where I could find him?"

A look of half surprise and half shock crossed the man's face, but a second later it was gone. He sat silent for a long moment before speaking again. "What'd ya say ya found?" he asked.

"I found something that belonged to him, I think. It had his name on it. It said 'for twenty five years of service, Superior Logging Company.'" Gil watched his face closely as he spoke the words. For a split second, the old man's eyes opened wide, then blinked a couple of times. *Was this man Joe Green?*

The old man rocked the chair back and stared into the trees across the street as if in deep thought. *What is he thinking? If I could only read his mind right now*, Gil thought.

Slowly the old man began to speak. "Don't know why I should believe ya. I guess ya jus look honest to me." Again he fell silent before continuing again. "I love the forest, been my whole life. Jus like to spend the rest of my life alone with my trees. Don't need any help. Never have. If'n a man don't get involved with others, he won't get disappointed."

Gil sensed a hint of bitterness in his voice, from some long ago incident.

"Ya say ya find something this Joe Green lost?" Without waiting for Gil to answer, he asked, "Where'd ya find it?"

"I found it in the lake," Gil pointed to the north. "While we were swimming."

The reaction was instant and explosive. "No! Couldn't be there! I know it couldn't be there." A look of distrust quickly overtook the man's face.

Gil knew he'd have to say the right thing quickly, or their conversation would be over. "But it had his name on it," Gil spoke firmly. "It was in a big glass canning jar. It looked like it'd been the lake for a long time," he pleaded for the old man to understand.

At Gil's words, the man's body slumped down into the chair and he stared at the ground, his head resting in his hands. Again he was silent.

Finally he spoke, "Joe Green couldn't have lost it in the lake. Wasn't on the lake."

"You did know Joe Green, then?"

"Did I say I knew Joe Green?" he snapped, then looked at the ground and said softly, "I'm sorry. Ya tell me something I don't wan'a hear." Slowly and softly he continued. "I'm Joe Green. I did have a watch. Company gave it to me. Put in a jar with my coins. My friend stole it. Said he was a Christian, then he stole my things."

"What about a locket with a woman's picture in it," Gil asked.

"My mother's locket? Ya found my mother's locket! That's the only picture I had of my mother." Tears welled up in the old man's eyes and he spoke again. "But that couldn't have been in the lake." He grew silent again, then finally spoke. "Ya give me too much to think about. Come back and see me in a day or two. I have to think about this."

"Sure Mr. Green, I'll come back in a couple of days and see you," Gil promised as he turned and headed back toward the depot.

CHAPTER X
COME HELP QUICK

e might be old," Gil told his friends as they headed back to the canoe. "But he's still pretty sharp. He seemed to think a friend of his had taken the things and ran off with it. Said he needed time to think," Gil explained.

A half hour later, they paddled into the cattails along the lake. "Glad to be done fighting that current," Jug puffed. "It sure has been a long time since lunch."

"Yes, it has," Gil agreed. Moments later, leaving the cattails, they turned the canoe toward the camp. "Hey, look on the right up ahead. The sheriff and his :friend must be out fishing."

As they drew closer to the boat, Jug called, "How's the fish biting?"

In answer, the sheriff held up a string of fish that they'd caught. "Doing alright.., he called. "You guys been ghost hunting again?' He laughed.

"We found a real one this afternoon," Gil responded.

"What do you mean?" The sheriff was serious now.

"You know, that Joe Green we told you about that used to live in Danesville. Well, he still does!"

"You mean that old fellow lives out in the woods all by himself?"

"That's right," Jug told him. "He's got a boat with a motor on it and goes down river to Hemlock Comers to get his supplies, we think."

"That's interesting," the sheriff replied. "What'd he say about the things you found?"

"Didn't want to believe it. He thought some one else had taken it," Gil explained. "We've got to go back and see him in a couple of days. We'll come in and get his things before we go back there."

"Tell you what," the sheriff offered. "We're going fishing again Monday. I'll pick up the old jar and bring it to you," he offered.

"Hey, that would be great," Gil responded. "Well, I guess we need to get back now. Have fun fishing."

Half awake, Gil rolled over in bed. He was thinking, *Why is Dad taking such a long shower? I know the shower is just on the other side of the wall, but why is it so noisy, and why is he taking it so early? KA-BOOM!* A clap of thunder shook the windows in the bunkhouse and Gil was suddenly wide awake.

He wasn't listening to his father taking a shower. He was in the bunkhouse listening to the rain beat down on the roof.

Gil checked his watch dial in the dim morning light. *Almost eight o'clock. Must really be overcast outside.* "Hey Jug. It's time to get up!" he called fumbling for the light switch.

"What do you mean, get up? It's still dark," he rubbed his eyes trying to get them accustomed to the bright light overhead.

"It's almost eight o'clock. We're going to be late for breakfast, and Uncle Jim wanted to go into town for church services today," Gil explained.

"Maybe he's changed his mind since he didn't get back from the Soo until after we went to bed," Jug suggested.

"That might be," Gil replied. "The trail out to the main road might be a little soggy with all this rain we've been getting."

Minutes later when they finished dressing, they slipped on their raincoats and ran for the kitchen.

Wow, it's wet out there," Gil stepped inside and stomped the water off his shoes, then hung his raincoat up on a peg to dry.

"We overslept," Jug called to Aunt Mary who was stirring something in a big bowl.

"Don't feel bad," she replied. "I guess we all did. The girls were sleeping pretty soundly, so we decided to let them sleep in. Jim said we'd just have our church services here today, with the rain and all."

"What can we do to help," Gil asked.

"I've got the pancake batter all ready. If you want to bake them, I'll fry some sausages and fix some scrambled eggs. You can set the table, Jug."

Breakfast was almost ready when Lori and Ann came in the door. "Why didn't you call us?" Lori asked.

"We didn't know it was morning, Ann told them. "It's so dark outside."

"We just felt so sorry for you girls that you'd had to work so hard here at camp," Jug told them. "We decided to let you off this morning," he spoke with *mock* sympathy dripping from his words.

"Oh, come on Jug," Ann shot back. "Just when did you ever feel sorry about us girls having to cook for you?" she laughed. "That does mean you're going to do the dishes too, doesn't it?"

Frank Austin

"Hey now," Jug cried out. "Don't push our kindness too far."

The downpour of rain slowed by the mid morning and finally stopped. "The radio weather report said it's going to clear up and we'll have a dry week ahead of us," Uncle Jim reported.

"I talked to the guys from our church yesterday," Jim continued. "The crew they're sending will leave there at noon this Friday, and they plan to be here before dark that evening. Some of them are going to install some plumbing in the kitchen, and get a bathroom working there."

"We have lumber here in the shed, and yesterday, I picked up the other supplies we'll need."

Gil awoke the next morning at the sound of a car driving into the campgrounds.

"It's the sheriff and his friend," Jug reported from the window. By the time they were dressed, the boat had started and seconds later, it took off with a roar and the sound gradually faded into the distance on the other side of the lake.

Later, Gil told Uncle Jim, "I can't believe it's almost noon." The morning had been a busy time, measuring. snapping chalk lines on the floor, and then sawing lumber and assembling the walls.

"Yes," Jim replied. "The morning did go quickly, but we got a lot done. Let's get cleaned up for lunch." Glancing toward the lake, Jug called. "Looks like the sheriff and his friend are done fishing and coming this way."

"Let's go see what they caught," Gil suggested. The two men were wearing the smile of success as they stepped out of the boat. The sheriff held up a stringer of good sized bass and called, "Caught these big fellows early this morning, then the perch and bluegills started biting."

"Haven't had so much fun since I was a little kid," the other man added."

"Don't let me forget," the sheriff spoke up. "I brought your jug of goodies out of my safe. Got it locked right there in my trunk."

"We'll give you a hand," Jim responded.

Aunt Mary appeared in the kitchen door just as the sheriff pulled the jar of coins out of his trunk. "I've got two extra plates set on the table, and dinner will be ready by the time you get washed up," she called.

"No, Mrs. West. We don't want to impose on you. We can just grab something in town."

"You'll do no such thing," she sputtered. "After being shut up in here with all that rain yesterday, we could use some news from the outside world."

Later as they sat eating, the sheriff spoke up, "We're going to do a little sightseeing this afternoon, so we won't need the boat until tomorrow evening at the earliest. If you'd take the boat down the creek until you hit the river, then you should be able to get right down to that ghost town without much effort."

"Oh, we wouldn't want to do that," Gil responded. "I'd be afraid we'd hurt your boat."

"Nonsense!" He said firmly. "I run it up and down the rivers lots of times during the year. I had it built for that kind of use, and if I find out you guys went over there in your canoe again, I'll lock you up in the county jail and throw away the key," he chuckled. He turned to Uncle Jim and said, "I showed the boys how to run the boat, and I'm serious about them taking it."

"Well, thank you," Uncle Jim replied. "I'll make sure they're careful with it."

The afternoon was warm and the bathroom project was dusty. Twenty minutes before it was time to eat, Jim called, "We're about done here, let's go jump in the lake and get some of this dirt off of us."

The cool water was refreshing as they plunged in and swam to the makeshift dock. "You guys want to take a quick trip over to see Mr. Green after we eat?"

"Sure, Jug answered.

"We'll go too," the girls agreed.

"I'd like to get the jar of things back to him as soon as we can," Gil told the others. "Something in the past was bothering him. I'd like to talk to him, now that he's had a little time to think about it."

A few minutes later, gathered around the table eating, Gil asked, "We were thinking about taking Mr. Green's things back to him Would it be alright to take the sheriff's boat and go over there after we're done eating?"

Jim checked his watch. "I guess we still have four hours of daylight left. I really don't want you to get locked up in jail the rest of the summer, so I guess it'd be alright, as long as you get back before dark."

"We'll be careful," Jug assured him.

"If you help carry the dishes to the kitchen when we're done eating, I'll help Mary wash them," he offered. "That will give you a few more minutes before dark."

"Oh, thank you Dad," she turned and gave him a big hug.

"I'll get the jar," Gil announced when the table had been cleared. "We'll need life jackets, and we'd better take a couple of flashlights just in case something happens."

"I think I'll put this jar in this cardboard box and stuff some papers around it so it doesn't get broken on the way." Gil set the jar in the box, then wadded up some papers and stuffed around it for padding. Picking up the box he called, "You guys about ready?"

"We're all set," the girls answered from the door.

"I've got the flashlights, so I guess I'm ready," Jug replied.

"Ok, let's get loaded."

Jug ran to the boat, jumped in and hit the starter, so it could warm up while the others loaded in and settled down in the seats.

"Everybody ready?" Jug asked.

"I think so," Gil replied and pushed the boat away from the shore.

Jug eased the throttle forward and the boat picked up speed as he circled around. "South shore, here we come," he yelled as the boat shot across the water.

"This sure beats a canoe," Lori cried above the noise of the motor.

It only seemed like a few seconds to Gil, when Jug slowed the motor and carefully guided the boat into the cattails "When we're coming back, that's when we'll really appreciate the motor doing the work," Jug called.

The creek wasn't deep enough to make time like they could on the lake, but still, it wasn't long before Jug called, "railroad grade just ahead," then swung the boat around the fallen tree.

Moving beyond the tree, Gil noticed the creek turned sharply to the east and moments later, joined the river. "Watch it," he called to Jug. "There may be some sand bars here where the streams join."

Just at that moment, Jug called, "Hang on!" and he took a sharp left turn quickly followed by a sharp right turn, then eased the boat into the center of the river.

Gil pulled the map from his pocket and spread it out on the seat beside him. "Looks like it's probably three of four miles down to the town. We want to watch for a stream that runs into the river not long after it turns back to the north. It's only about a half mile to the town after that."

The river was deeper, so they could make better time. Jug eased the throttle off on the bends and speeded up on the straight stretches. Several minutes later the stream swung to the west for a couple of miles and then turned in a more northerly direction. "That stream should be coming up soon," Gil warned them.

A hundred yards farther Gil called, "That's the stream. Now pretty soon we'll start to head back west, and that's where the ghost town should be."

Jug slowed the motor as the river turned west again and moved close to the right side.

Gil carefully studied the shoreline. The river bank was surprisingly free of low brush where the big trees overspread the river. "According to the map, that little spring should be right in here somewhere," he told the others.

Halfway around the bend he noticed a clump of bushes growing right down to the waters edge. Gil was about to dismiss it as nothing, when suddenly, he saw a narrow opening in the middle of it.

"Hold up!" He called pointing to the passage in the brush. "Let's take a look at that."

Jug careful eased the boat into the brush and suddenly, there was Mr. Green's dock.

"Pull up behind the canoe, and tie the boat to the dock,', Gil instructed. Stepping out, he secured the boat and called to Lori, "Would you hand me the box with the jar in it?"

Lori handed him the box, then climbed out on the dock. "Should we all go with you?" She asked.

"Why don't I go on ahead first, and then if everything's alright, I'll motion for you to come," Gil suggested. He waited for the others to get as close to the house as possible without being seen, then moved down the path toward the house.

Cradling the box in his left arm, he walked to the porch, then stepped up and knocked on the door frame. Hearing nothing, he repeated the knock. *Maybe he didn't hear,* he thought. Reaching out, he pulled the screen door open and knocked loudly on the door. Suddenly, at the third knock, the door swung in.

Caught off guard, Gil called, "Mr. Green, are you home?" No answer. *His boat is here, he must be around here somewhere,* he thought. "Mr. Green! Mr. Green, are you in there?"

Still no sound. Then all at once, he heard something. Again, he called in the door, "Mr. Green, are you in there?" He leaned close to the door and listened intently.

"Don't hurt me---," a weak voice moaned from inside the house.

Gil quickly pushed the door open and stepped inside calling, "Mr. Green, are you hurt?"

"Don't hurt me anymore," the voice moaned from the back of the house. "Just leave me alone," then it was silent.

Quickly, Gil moved toward the sound. Entering what appeared to be the kitchen, he discovered the old man laying on the floor. His face was bruised and his nose was bloody. His breathing was slow and labored and now and then a moan would escape from his lips. Better get help quick, Gil turned and hurried to the front door. Stepping out on the porch, he waved to his friends and called, "Come help me! Quick! Mr. Green's been hurt." Then he turned and hurried back to the old man.

"Mr. Green," he knelt down, "What happened?"

"No! No! Don't hurt me anymore," he pulled away from Gil.

"Mr. Green, we're not going to hurt you. We're going to help you," he said firmly.

"Don't hurt me," the old man begged. "I'll tell ya where my money is," his voice faded and he slumped back.

Just then his three friends hurried into the room. "What happened?" Jug cried.

"Get a blanket and a pillow," Gil ordered. "See if you can find a pan of cold water and some cloths to put on his head."

Seconds later, Lori returned with a pan of water and began to sponge the dirt and blood from his face, then she dipped a wash cloth and placed it on his forehead.

Gil took the blanket from Jug and covered the old man, then slipped a pillow carefully under his head. Slowly the old man began to relax as they worked over him, and the moaning stopped as he slept.

"What should we do?" Lori asked. Aunt Mary is a nurse, do you think we should go for help?"

"By the looks of his face, they must have beat on him pretty hard," Jug spoke up. "I think I ought to go get Aunt Mary!"

"It'd be a good idea," Gil answered. "We can't tell anything other than how he looks, and he looks pretty beat up. Somebody must have been trying to rob him. He said something about money, and not hurting him any more."

"If you go get Aunt Mary, maybe she can tell us if he needs to go to the hospital, or not. "Take Ann with you. You'll need someone to watch for rocks and sandbars."

"Ok," Jug replied and they stood up and headed toward the door.

"Better tie something on those bushes by the dock so you can spot it from the river," Gil told them.

Spotting a bright orange plastic hunters vest hanging by the door, Jug grabbed it and they headed out the door toward the river.

Gil and Lori continued working over Joe trying to make him comfortable. As the minutes ticked by slowly, he began to stir a little.

Gil leaned close and spoke to him, "Mr. Green. What happened? Why did they try to beat you up?"

"Where am I?" He groaned and his eyes flickered open. "Who are ya?" He asked. "Don't hurt me," his eyes closed and he fell into sleep again.

Lori changed the cloth on his forehead again and moments later, his eyes opened. "Feeling better?" She asked.

"Who are ya?" He whispered to Lori, "Are you an angel?"

"We've come to help you, Gil told him. "Remember, I came and talked to you a couple of days ago about some of things that we found in the lake."

Momentarily, a look of doubt appeared on the wrinkled face, then all at once it disappeared. "I remember ya-- -,"his voice trailed off into sleep.

Gil took the old man's wrist and checked his pulse. "It's strong, just a little fast," he reported.

"How long do you think he's been laying here?" Lori whispered.

"Might have been a half hour. Blood was dry on his face, but it couldn't have happened very long ago. I guess there's not much more we can do for him right now," Gil added softly.

"I'm going to see if I can find some soup or something we could give him when he wakes up," Lori suggested. Standing up, she began to look around the room. The kitchen looked like a picture cut out of an old magazine, but it was as clean and tidy as it could be. She found a can of chicken soup in one cupboard and a pan in another. Minutes later, the aroma of the soup filled the kitchen and the old timer stirred again.

"Feeling any better?" Gil inquired when Joe opened his eyes.

He struggled to move, then groaned and settled back on the floor. Slowly he spoke, "Those guys really worked me over. Followed me when I came back from town. Wanted my money. Took what I had in my pocket. Wasn't much. Wanted more money. Why they think I'd keep a lot of money here in the woods?"

"I fixed some soup for you," Lori spoke to him "Feel like eating some? We can prop you up on some pillows."

"Don't know why ya is helping me," he spoke softly. "I don't even know ya."

"We're Christians," Lori told him. "We're supposed to help others."

Suddenly, the old man grew silent and Gil could detect a tear in his eye. "I'm going to try to raise your shoulders and Lori will put some pillows under you."

"Ya don't have to help me," he protested. "I'll be alright tomorrow."

"Here, try some of this," Lori raised the spoon to his lips.

After eating some of the soup, the old man began to perk up a little. "Can't understand how ya found me."

"Remember, I was here a couple of days ago and talked to you?" Gil explained. "I said we'd come back in a couple days with the things we found in the lake. Well we came down the river in a boat, and found you hurt and laying on the floor."

Joe grew silent again, as if a door to the past had been opened and he didn't want to look in. "Could ya help me up on the couch?" He pointed toward a blanket covered sofa in the other room. "Sure, if you think you're up to it," Gil answered grabbing him under his shoulders and lifting. Together, with Lori's help on the other arm they were able to get him settled on the couch.

"Two of our friends were with us, but we sent them back to the logging camp to get my Aunt Mary," Gil told him. "She's a nurse and she can check you over to see if anything is broken. They should be back here pretty soon."

"Do you know who did this to you?" Lori questioned.

"Couple of *no goods* that hang around the bar in town. Too lazy to work - - -,"his voice trailed off as he slipped into sleep.

Frank Austin

"Poor old man," Lori responded, covering him with a blanket. It's a wonder they didn't kill him."

Sitting down to wait for the boat to return, Gil looked around the room. It was spotless. The hardwood floor shone like it had just been refinished. The rest of in the room appeared as if it had been dropped there from the first half of the last century.

Several paintings of birds and wildlife were hanging on the walls around the room. "They look so alive that you could reach out and touch them," Lori commented.

Gil stood up and walked to the nearest picture, taking a closer look. "Hey, it's signed Joe in the comer. Do you think he might have painted them?"

"I think probably he did," Lori replied. "There's a half finished painting over there in that room." She pointed to an open door.

On the couch, Joe stirred again and said, "They thought they'd killed me. Hit me in the belly an' knocked the wind out'ta me. Got scared an' run."

All at once the old man slipped his feet off the couch and tried to sit up. But then, just as suddenly his face turned white and he got a funny look in his eyes. "Mr. Green, you'd better lay back down. You're just not strong enough to sit up yet."

Lori's voice seemed to calm him and he settled back down on the couch. "Guess ye're right. I'm kin'da shaky yet."

"Listen," Gil spoke up. "Sounds like the boat is coming." He stood and stepped outside to wait. A few seconds later, three people emerged from the bushes by the river.

"How's he doing?" Jug called as he hurried toward the house.

"Seems to be doing better, but he really took quite a beating for a man his age," Gil replied.

Entering the house once more, Gil walked close to the old man and said, "This is my Aunt Mary. She's a nurse, and she can check you over to see if anything is broken."

"Don't need to bother with me," the old man sputtered. "I'll be alright in the morning."

"Nonsense, Mr. Green. It looks like you've taken quite a beating." She pulled a stethoscope from her bag and listened to his heart. "Ok, that sounds pretty good," she told him.

"How long has it been since you saw a doctor?" She asked as she continued to check him over.

"Don't know," he answered. "Old Doc Morgan lived 'cross the street til he got pneumonia an died five or six years ago. Haven't needed a doctor since then."

"Everybody else moved on when they took the tracks out, 'cept me an' Doc. Didn't have a family, nobody to go to. So we just stayed here. Wife died years ago," he rambled on.

"Well Mr. Green, you came through that beating very well for a man your age. I'm going to put something on some of these bruises, and I want you to take it easy for a few days. If you feel like it in the morning, I'll have the boys bring you over to the logging camp. You can stay with us until you get recovered."

"No, no, no," he protested. "I'll get by."

"Now, Mr. Green. You're in no shape to cook for yourself, and I have to get three meals every day for these hungry kids anyway. One more mouth to feed won't make any difference," she told him as she prepared to leave.

"Ok, Mr. Green." Gil spoke up. "Jug is going to take the ladies back to the logging camp now, but I'm going to stay here with you tonight. I want to make sure that those two men don't come back to rob you."

"No, no," he protested again, but Gil sensed that the old man did want him to stay.

CHAPTER XI
IT JUST CAN'T BE

The old man slept for fifteen minutes after the others had gone. Meanwhile Gil prepared for the darkness that was fast approaching. He lit an oil lamp in the kitchen and two in the living room. Seeing a shotgun leaning up in one corner of the room, his thoughts turned to the two men that had been there that afternoon. *Better find some shells for that gun, just to be safe. And I guess I'd better block the doors so they won't be able to get in there.* Looking around, he found some shells for the gun, and wedged a couple of chairs under the doorknobs so the doors couldn't be opened from the outside.

There, that ought to do it, he told himself walking back into the living room.

"What's in the box?" The old timers voice startled him.

"What box? Oh, you mean this one." Gil nodded his head toward the box containing the old jar. "That's what I found in the lake."

"If ya pump up that gas lantern and light it, maybe we can see better. And there's some tea bags in the kitchen. If ya could fix me a cup a tea, I'd like ta take a look at the things ya found." The old man told him.

Gil went to the kitchen and put some water on to heat, then

returned to the other room to get the gas lamp prepared. By the time he had finished with it, the teakettle was singing in the kitchen. "I'll go fix your tea, and then we can take a look at the jar."

When Gil returned with the tea, the old man was sitting up on the couch.

"Put it right here," he motioned to a small table at the end of the couch.

Gil slid another low table in front of Joe and said, "I'll set the things right here so they're handy for you," he told him. Pulling the packing papers out of the box, he lifted the jar and placed it on the table.

"Does this look familiar?" Gil asked as he lifted the wire bail holding the lid in place.

Knowing that his hand wouldn't fit inside of the jar, he tipped it up and carefully poured some of the contents on the table.

"Here's what I wanted you to see," he told him as he reached for the cloth wrapped objects.

"See this?" he unwrapped the old watch and handed it to the old timer.

The old man's eyes went wide, "It just can't be," he shook his head. "They couldn't have been in the lake. Had ta be some one else's." He turned the watch in his hand and flipped the cover open. His eyebrows dropped, and tears began to appear in his eyes as he read the inscription. "It can't be mine, but it is."

Gil unwrapped the locket and held it out to him. Joe stared at it for a moment before he took it, almost like he was afraid to touch it but couldn't resist. He slowly studied the locket then flipped it open. Again, a look of surprise came over him and a couple of tears ran down his face.

Slowly and softly he spoke, "I jus can't believe it. This is the only picture I had of my mother. 'Fore I was married, I boarded out at the logging camp. Tryin' ta save some money so I could get married." Suddenly, the old man grew silent like he was still trying to figure things out.

"I've ben such a fool!" he cried out all at once. "Many years ago, a young feller worked with me at the camp. Liked 'im a lot. Said he was a Christian. Kept tellin' me I should be one too. Almost convinced me. Then one night he came up missin' an so did my jar of savin's. Just couldn't believe my friend took it, but the evidence seemed to point to 'im."

"I thought, if that's the way a Christian is, then I don't wan'a be one. Couple years later he came back ta see me. Said his mother had a heart attack. He had to go take care of her. I thought it was just an excuse. Thought 'is conscience was just bothering 'im."

"When ya come here the other day. Said ya found the things, I just couldn't believe it. Couldn't be possible. It bothered me, that ya knew so much about it. Couldn't be just a lucky guess. I just didn't want it to be true. I'd blamed my friend so long, I just didn't wan'a admit I was wrong. Problem was, I'd overlooked somethin' important."

"Was another young feller stayin' at camp. Come up missin' 'bout the same time. Was a misfit. Didn't like ta work. Was in the spring. The ice on the lake was soft. When he try to cross the ice ta get away must have fell in and drown right where ya find the jar. Found 'im a few days later. Body washed up on shore. I just never thought bout 'im takin' the jar."

"The train come in every day to the copper mine across the lake. Had to take the ore out. Must have ben headin' cross the lake ta take the train when he fell through the ice."

Hesitating, he sat there with the watch in one hand, and the locket in the other, staring at the floor. Finally he continued. "I've ben such a fool all these years. Ol' Doc Morgan kep' tellin' me I should quit bein' so bitter and repent of my sins and get saved. He was a good man. Lived just like the Bible says, but I was just too stubborn to give in."

He picked up the locket and studied the picture. "She used ta read me stories from the Bible every day," the old man mused. "Then she'd pray fur me. Prayed I'd be saved. I was such a fool!"

"You know, Mr. Green, it's not too late for you to be saved. You can ask Jesus right now to forgive your sins and to come into your heart. He loves you so much that he died in your place and my place to save us from the penalty of our sins. His blood can wash away all of your sins," Gil explained.

"Are ya sure it's not too late?" Joe asked.

"It's not too late," Gil assured him. "Jesus wants you to be part of his family right now."

Slowly the old man bowed his head and in stumbling words confessed his sins and asked Jesus to save him.

When he had finished praying, he spoke, "Livin' in the woods and seein' God's creation all around me, I knew my mother was right. I knew old Doc had somethin' that I needed, but I was too stubborn to admit that I needed someone ta help me. Thought I could take care of myself When those two fellers beat me up, I was scared for the first time in my life."

It was six o'clock and the birds were chirping their wake up calls. Gil rubbed his eyes and looked around. The old man was still sleeping soundly, but the rising sun was already painting a golden glow in the eastern sky. It wouldn't be long before the boat would return, and Mr. Green would need something to eat.

Rising quietly, he went to the kitchen and looked around to see what he could make for breakfast. Eggs, bacon, and pancake mix. I *think breakfast won 't be too difficult*, he thought. Grabbing a frying pan, he set it on a burner and began to prepare breakfast.

Fifteen minutes later Joe called from the doorway, "You're making some pretty good smells, for a young feller."

"Looks like you're feeling better this morning?" Gil replied.

"I'm kinda sore. Feel a lot better'n last night."

"I've got some breakfast about ready. I set a couple of plates there at the table. Just pull up a chair, and it'll be ready in a minute."

Joining the old man at the table, Gil told him, "I expect the others to be back with the boat before long. If you feel strong enough, we'll take you back to the camp until you get strong enough to come back here."

Gil could see that he was stronger this morning, but his eyes were swollen and turning black around them. He really wasn't ready to be on his own yet.

"Ben thinkin,'" Joe spoke up as they began eating. " Ya know, I sold my land a long time ago to an old friend who owned a loggin company. He bought what was left of the town so he'd have a place to get away from the big city. Wanted me to keep the buildin's up enough so they wouldn't fall down. He'd come and stay every summer for a while with Doc and me. We'd have a good time talkin' 'bout the good old days here in Danesville. Then fifteen years ago he got killed in a car accident. Hadn't had any visitors since, til ya come along."

"I put the money in the bank when I sold the land, and it didn't take much for me to live on here in the woods. With my pension, I get along good. Got a big pile of money built up in the bank, and no where to spend it."

Bang, Bang, Bang. Someone was pounding on the front door. "I'll get it," Gil jumped up and ran to the door. He quickly pulled the chair away and swung the door open.

"Bout time you answered," Jug stepped inside and motioned for the girls to follow.

"How's Mr. Green?" Lori inquired.

"I'm doin' much better this mornin'," Joe called from the kitchen door. "This young feller here cooked me a good breakfast. Just need to take care of a few dishes an we'll be ready ta go."

"We'll get them," Ann called and the girls headed for the kitchen. "You just sit down and take it easy."

"Need ta take a few things with me," he said and disappeared into another room. A couple minutes later he returned and sat down on the couch, then told the boys, "I'm goin' ta keep the watch an locket for now. They mean a lot ta me. Don't really hav any need for the coins. I want ya young folks ta hav 'um."

It was breakfast time the next morning when the sheriff and his friend appeared in the dining room door at the camp.

"Breakfast ready yet?" He called out as he entered the room.

"Jug ate almost everything," Gil replied. "But I'm sure we can scrape up something for you.

"And how are you doing this morning, Mr. Green?" The sheriff asked.

"No more of this Mr. stuff," the old man scolded the sheriff. "My name is just plain Joe to ya folks. These folks are so nice ta me. Hardly let me do anythin for myself. They're spoilin' me. Won't wana go back ta my shack in the woods."

"I know what you mean," the sheriff agreed. "This here is the best restaurant in the county! By the way, Joe. We caught those two guys that beat you up. We searched their room and found a lot of stolen stuff. After the judge gets done with them, they won't bother anyone for a long time."

"If someone had jus taken time to set them two fellers on the right path, a long time ago," Joe spoke up. Could ha' made a difference in their lives. Ya know, Sheriff: bein' here has brought back a lot of memories for me. Thinkin' bout these kids from the cities bein' able to come out here, an see all the greatness of God's creation. Could change their lives."

"I'm old and worn out. But there's a pile of money in my bank account. I wana use it to help kids tum out like these four kids sitin' here at this table. I want these kids ta hav' a good education. I've wasted too many years now, but what time I have left, I wana do something useful!"

Tears welled up in Gil's eyes. *His father had been right. God truly had supplied his needs. Thank you Lord, forgive me my lack of faith.*

The heavens are thine, the earth also is thine:
as for the world and the fulness thereof,
thou hast founded them. Psa. 89:11

The End

CPSIA information can be obtained
at www.ICGtesting.com
Printed in the USA
BVHW041827050521
606581BV00022B/370

9 781973 692607